VAN BUREN DISTRICT LIBRARY
DECATUR

P9-DFO-418

DISCARDED

A BULLET
FOR BILLY

Center Point
Large Print

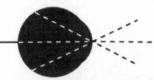

**This Large Print Book carries the
Seal of Approval of N.A.V.H.**

A BULLET
FOR BILLY

BILL
BROOKS

CENTER POINT LARGE PRINT
THORNDIKE, MAINE

LP
Bro

This Center Point Large Print edition is published
in the year 2013 by arrangement with
Golden West Literary Agency.

Copyright © 2007 by Bill Brooks.

All rights reserved.

This book is a work of fiction. Names, characters, places,
and incidents are products of the author's imagination or
are used fictitiously and are not to be construed as real.
Any resemblance to actual events, locales, organizations,
or persons, living or dead, is entirely coincidental.

The text of this Large Print edition is unabridged.
In other aspects, this book may
vary from the original edition.
Printed in the United States of America
on permanent paper.
Set in 16-point Times New Roman type.

ISBN: 978-1-61173-619-9

Library of Congress Cataloging-in-Publication Data

Brooks, Bill, 1943–
A bullet for Billy / Bill Brooks.
pages ; cm.
ISBN 978-1-61173-619-9 (library binding)
1. Young women—Crimes against—Fiction. 2. Murderers—Fiction.
    3. Prisoners—Mexico—Fiction. 4. Large type books. I. Title.
PS3552.R65863B85 2013
813´.54—dc23
                                                                      2012035519

'|13
center
point

For Bob Faulkner,
writer, pal, muleskinner,
and a pretty good man
to go upriver with, I'm betting.

A BULLET
FOR BILLY

Chapter One

You couldn't hear it falling, but you could tell from the rattling wind and the cold creeping in under the door that it had snowed the night before. I rose and put on a pot of Arbuckle after hopping into my pants and boots.

Luz was still asleep in the bed. I was tempted to stay in there with her. She had a warmth that made me want to be lazy and playful.

I rubbed frost from inside the window and looked out at the horses that were strutting around in the corral blowing steam from their nostrils. The buckskin stud was boxed off from the mares, and he was nickering and daring them to kick down the rails.

I put on a wool shirt and threw some more chunks of wood into the stove's belly. I tried to be quiet about it, but Luz rose to one elbow and smiled.

"You hungry?" she said.

"When am I not?" I said.

She came out from town once a week to clean and keep me a little company. That's how it began. She was the widow of a man who broke his neck from falling under a wagon he'd been loading with bricks. The workhorses spooked just enough to roll the wheel over him. From everything she'd told me about him, he was a good man but full of bad luck. She had two half-grown children her sister watched on the nights she spent with me.

She started to get out of bed.

"Why don't you let me get you some coffee," I said. "I'll make the breakfast too."

She liked to switch from English to Spanish when we talked, and over time I'd learned quite a bit of her language. Now she smiled and said in her own language, "*Me siento como soy una esposa otra vez.*"

"Yes, it feels like you're my wife too," I said. "It's not so bad, is it, to feel like that?"

"But when you cook for me," she said in English this time, "it is like you are my wife." Then she laughed and brushed away the hair that had fallen over one side of her face and tucked it behind her ear.

"Why didn't you ever remarry?" I said, mixing some flour and water and a little yeast for biscuits.

"I don't know," she said. "I guess the same reason you never did."

"I've never been married," I said.

"So you said. But the question is, why not?"

I shrugged.

"Just never got around to it, I guess."

She shrugged.

"Now you know why I didn't remarry, too busy, too much work. And besides, all the hombres who aren't married are either old or have buck teeth." She laughed again.

She had straight black hair she normally kept parted down the center and twisted into braids or wrapped atop her head and held with large combs. But when her work around my place was finished and we'd sit down to have supper, she'd unpin or unbraid her hair and let it all fall free, and it made her look younger and more at ease, and I think she knew it and that's why she did it.

Over the weeks we'd flirt and eat. The flirting with each other began about the fourth or fifth time she'd come out to clean. She had a friendly way about her and was always singing softly while she worked. But when I talked to her I could tell she always kept something back—like a gambler with a pretty good hand, but not necessarily the *best* hand at the table.

She'd be in the house doing something and I'd be out on the porch mending a broken stirrup or just having a cup of coffee, and she'd come out and ask if she could get me anything and we'd just get to talking. Then she told me about her husband, how he'd died, and I could see that even after three years she was still affected by the loss—the way her bottom lip quivered sometimes when she talked about him. She would apologize

11

as if she had something to be sorry for. I told her she didn't and she could talk to me about anything that she wanted to.

"He was a good husband and a father . . . ," she said that first time. I remember how the light from the setting sun turned her brown skin golden, how it caused her eyes to shine like wet black stones. I kept on thinking about her long after she headed home and finally decided I didn't want the day with her to end so soon, and so worked up the courage to ask her to stay and have supper with me. I thought for sure she'd turn me down, make some excuse as to why she had to get back to town to take care of her kids. But she stayed, telling me that her sister, Carmelita, watched her children when she went off to clean houses.

We'd carry my small table outside and eat our supper there because the weather was warm and pleasant. I found some candles and set them atop the table and we ate with just the light from them. We started out sitting at opposite ends of the table and ended up sitting next to each other, the third or fourth time we ate together.

She asked me to tell her about myself and I probably talked way too much—more than I had with anyone about my own past. I told her I'd once been a Texas Ranger but I didn't tell her why I'd quit. I told her about herding cattle up some of the trails from Texas into Kansas and once into New Mexico, which is how I'd come to eventually settle here. But I never told her about the ranch owner's wife in Nebraska and why I finally left that job. I told her lots of things but not everything.

"I did a lot of drifting," I said. "But I always liked this country best and knew someday I'd come back. And, well, here I am."

"I was wondering what brought you here," she said.

"Now you know."

One other thing I never told her about me was that I'd most recently killed a man named Johnny Waco—now nearly a year ago in the history book of my life. Everyone in Coffin Flats knew about it at the time, and why I had done it. But she lived out nearer to Wild Horse River than Coffin Flats, and if she did know about it, she never brought it up in our conversations, and I appreciated that about her.

Her laughter was something to behold. She was beautiful when she laughed. She was no young girl and her age and looks, by most men's standards, probably put her in the average category, I guess you'd say. And being a widow with children didn't exactly endear her to the few eligible bachelors worth a peck when there were so many younger, fairer Mexican women whose folks wanted to see them married off down in this part of the country. But what Luz was, was just about right for me at this time of my life. That first night we had supper together I rode with her back to her home. She had a little paint mare. She insisted she could make it home by herself just fine like she was accustomed to doing, but I now felt an obligation to make sure she got home safe and sound.

We both knew something had changed in our relationship that night—that if she continued coming out to the house and we continued along the same lines it was going to be more than just her cleaning my house and more than just us having supper together.

We got to her front door, the night having long descended, the inside of the casita dark, and we just sat there for a moment.

"What do you want from me, Señor Glass?" she finally said.

"Nothing, Luz."

She gave me long enough to explain it.

"I don't know," I said. "I liked tonight, having supper with you, talking, laughing, telling you about myself. I like the fact you smoke cigarettes even though I never have, but I'm thinking of taking up the habit. I like the way the evening sun looks in your eyes. I don't know what it all means. I just know I liked it and wouldn't mind if we made it a regular deal."

"I liked it too," she said. "But what might people say?"

"Hell, I don't care if you don't. We're both still

14

vital people, me and you, Luz. You're widowed and I'm single; what can they say that's so terrible?"

She touched my hand for the first time and I leaned and kissed her soft cheek.

"Then I'll see you next week," I said.

"Yes, you'll see me next week."

So that's how it began, like that—two strangers who'd come to know each other a little more each time over the ensuing weeks and decided at some point we didn't want to stop with just supper.

When the coffee was ready I poured her a cup, remembering she liked two spoonfuls of sugar in hers, and brought it to her and said, "I'm going to go out and break ice off the water troughs for the horses, then gather some eggs if those chickens didn't all get et last night by the coyotes and we'll have some eggs and biscuits with honey for breakfast, how will that be?"

"In bed?"

"Sure. We'll pretend we're rich people."

She reached up and kissed me, letting the blanket drop away when she did, her warm brown breasts pressed against me as she hugged my neck. And it roused my desire all over again.

"Don't go anywhere," I said. "I'll be right back."

The horses pricked their ears at my approach and I took the hand ax and busted the plates of ice off their water and said, "There you are, ladies." The stud stood off watching me cautiously as I went to his pen. I shattered the ice on his water and said, "Just so you know, we're going to have us another go-round today, so you might just as well get used to the idea."

He tossed his head and pawed the cold earth just as if he knew what I was talking about. The thought of getting bucked off on such a cold morning was a little more than I wanted to think about. I'd wait till around midmorning, then give it a go—when it was a little warmer and the ground not so damn hard.

I went over to the chicken coop—one I'd constructed myself and surrounded with chicken wire but didn't seem to do much good when it came to crafty coyotes and zealous badgers. Even had a hawk once that flew down and took one. I strung more chicken wire for a barrier. Those chickens acted scared and I couldn't blame them. I unlatched the wire holding the small gate so I could enter and hopefully find a few eggs for breakfast. The rooster squawked like someone told him he was about to be murdered and the hens ran about with their clipped wings flapping and squawking too.

Then I saw something way out on the road that caused me to pause: a quarter-top leather buggy, black against the snow, pulled by a single trotter. I didn't know anybody in Coffin Flats who owned such a rig except the new doctor. I wondered what the hell the new doctor was headed to my place for.

I got my eggs, holding them in the fold of my shirttails, and hitched the gate shut again and started up to the house. Inside I set the eggs in a bowl on the sideboard next to the stove and said to Luz, "Someone's coming. Looks like that new doctor. Maybe you ought to get dressed. You know I'm a jealous man."

She smiled boldly, said, "Oh, you are, huh."

"Maybe just a little."

"I like that you are," she said.

She tossed back the covers and stood fully naked before me, her arms out away from her sides.

"You're a sight and a half, woman. And if you keep that up, I'm going to crawl back in the bed with you, and that new doctor will just have to wait outside till we're done in here."

She laughed and came and threw her arms around my neck and kissed my mouth.

"Okay," she said. "I'll get dressed, and I'll make breakfast too."

I stepped out on the porch, closing the door behind me.

But the man riding in the hack wasn't the new doctor. Instead it was a man I hadn't seen in almost two years and never thought I'd see again.

His name was Gus Rogers, Captain Gus Rogers, and I knew he hadn't traveled all the way from Texas just to pay a social visit.

He halted the hack, the morning sun glistening in the new snowfall, his horse blowing steam.

"Jim," he said in that South Texas drawl of his as he just sat there huddled inside a mackinaw with his hat pulled down tight to the top of his ears.

"Cap'n," I said. "You're quite a ways from home."

"Hell if I ain't, old son."

"You lost, or just out wandering the earth?"

He smiled like a man who didn't do it much.

"Neither," he said. "I come looking for you."

"Get on down," I said. "Was about to have some breakfast. You hungry?"

"No, not too much. Could use a taste of hot coffee though, maybe just a finger or two of something in it to ward off the chill."

I watched the way he stepped out of the hack; like a man who had something in him broken.

He stood for a moment straightening himself, hands pressed to his back, looking around.

"Nice little place you got here," he said.

"Ain't it though."

"Never thought I'd see the day Jim Glass had himself a house." He looked to the corral. "Nice horses too. Hell, old son, you've become like some sort of potentate."

"Hardly," I said. I was trying to kill enough time for Luz to slip on a dress but I figured by now she had. I almost smiled at the thought of the look on the Cap'n's face was he to see her innocent beauty in all its glory, a man like him, who was all Bible and by the book.

"Let's get in out of this morning cold. Coffee's already on," I said.

I waited for him to go first and saw the way he was listing and moving slow. I'd known the man for a goodly number of years, knew him to always be tough as a blackjack stump, figured even bullets couldn't kill him, which they hadn't yet after being shot at least three times I knew about.

His face was ashen, his features drawn, and he looked like he had aged twenty years since I'd last seen him.

I introduced him to Luz and told him to take a seat at the table. He gave her an appraising eye and smiled like a coon eating melon.

"Ma'am," he said, touching the brim of his Stetson with a finger. Supporting most of his weight on the back of the chair and edge of the table, he eased himself down.

I went to the cupboard and took out the bottle of bourbon I kept there for special occasions, which were mostly for the nights after Luz and I had supper together and would sit out on the porch and watch the sun set and sip and talk till it got dark. She confessed she quite liked the taste of my whiskey.

I poured the Cap'n a cup of coffee, then poured in some of the whiskey till he waved a hand over the cup. "Good enough," he said.

Luz threw together our breakfast but he just let his plate sit in front of him, trying to be polite, but only picking at it, saying, "This is real good, ma'am."

I could tell by the look on Luz's face she had several questions but knew to wait to ask them. Finally she took up our plates and cleaned them, then put on her wrap and said, "I have to be going, Jim. I'll see you next week."

I walked her out to her little horse and helped her up after a long good-bye kiss.

"Who is that man?" she asked.

"Just somebody from my past," I said.

"He looks sick."

"I'll see you next week then?" I said.

She looked at me in a way that made me wonder if everything they said about a woman's intuition wasn't true.

"Whoever he is or whatever his problem, he feels like trouble," she said.

"Not far as I'm concerned," I said.

"I'll bring some silk flowers for the grave, next time I come," she said.

"That would be nice."

She clucked the little horse to a start, and I stood and watched her head back toward Coffin Flats.

I went back inside dreading whatever it was that had brought Cap'n Gus Rogers to my front door on a fresh winter day.

Chapter Two

"Nice lady, your friend," the Cap'n said when I stepped back inside.

"Yeah, you want a refill of that Arbuckle?"

He held out his cup and I filled it with coffee, then my own, and set the pot back atop the stove plate. He looked at the bottle of bourbon.

"Help yourself, Cap'n," I said.

He spilled in a nice portion and stirred it with his spoon and sipped it.

"So you want to tell me why you came all the way from Texas?"

He took his time sipping the coffee, blowing off the steam, and said, "Thank Jesus for the whiskey 'cause you still can't make coffee worth a holy damn, Jim."

"Kinda early to be drinking, isn't it?"

He arched his back as though it was aching, then relaxed. He had lost weight since I'd last seen him, though he never was a big man to begin with: maybe a hundred fifty, tops, but a solidly built man of good coloration and clear keen eyes that seemed to see everything at a glance. Now he was down to a lot less and looking gaunt, his gray eyes sunk back inside their sockets under a ridge of forehead. His cheeks were sunk in and his color an unhealthy pale.

"I came to ask you a favor and you know I don't ever ask them easy," he said.

"Yes sir, I know that."

He looked uncomfortable.

"You okay, Cap'n?"

"Depends which day it is. Today's worse than yesterday was."

"What's the favor?" I said.

He looked grim.

"Got me this real bad problem, Jim. First thing you should know is, I'm dying. Doctors tell me I got five, maybe six weeks left at the outside . . ."

"Sorry to hear that," I said, and I truly was. The Cap'n was one of the best men I'd ever met in my life. He waved a hand.

"Didn't come looking for pity, just need to tell you this so you'll know why I come this far and what I come for."

"Go on with it," I said.

"You remember I got two grandboys?"

"Seems to me I do."

"Billy Edward, he's the oldest, and Sam Houston is five years younger, nineteen and fourteen."

I faintly remembered him speaking of them when I rangered for him.

"They're my Laura Lee's kids, and as you know she's my only child. Never had no boys of my own, just Laura Lee. Had her, then JoAnn died right after and I never married again because there was no use to it. You love a woman as hard as I loved JoAnn, well, what's the use of trying to find something to compete with that. I raised Laura Lee best as I could and she turned out a good woman with poor judgment when it came to men.

"Went through two marriages herself before she met the right man. That's how come the difference in her boys' ages. Billy was fathered by her first husband, Wayne Brown, and Sam was fathered by her second, Orville Cutter. Anyway, neither of them was much count and took off soon as they found out she was pregnant. Then she met this Jardine Frost fellow. They were living together over in Tascosa, her and this Jardine raising the boys together, Jardine adopted them and gave them his last name. From what she'd written me, Jardine was a good, decent man, hard worker, and treated her boys like they were his own, she said. Then he got himself killed in a dispute over a horse."

Cap'n Rogers told it with his eyes cast down, remembering it all, and when he mentioned about this Jardine Frost getting killed, he just shook his head slowly.

"Well," he said, sipping from his cup, "like I said, Laura Lee never did have any luck with men, good or bad. Frost getting himself killed just about done it as far as those boys standing a chance of getting raised right. They just went wild after he passed. I'm sure she did her best to raise them right, but you know when boys don't have no father to discipline them, they can get off the track real fast.

"I didn't learn about a lot of this till later on—till after it was too late for me to do anything about it. Not that there was much I might could have done living three hundred miles away at the time. But maybe if she'd come lived with me and brought those boys with her, I could have been some sort of father to them and taught them the right thing to do . . ."

He looked pained and he drank down more of the whiskey-laced coffee, and I wasn't sure I wanted to hear more of this story because it just felt like it wasn't going to get any better the more of it he told.

He looked up at me with those gray eyes, and I didn't see in them what I once had: a man too tough to be whipped. What I saw now was a man who had five, six weeks at the outside to live and peck of personal problems.

"The way it turned out was Billy and Sam drifted off and started getting themselves to doing bad stunts."

"What sort of bad stunts?" I said.

"Mostly minor stuff at first—gambling, drinking, fighting, petty thievery. But like most wild boys who start out slow, they did not stay that

24

way. Pretty darn soon they progressed up the ranks to become true outlaws—stealing cattle and horses and even got accused of robbing a bank in Las Vegas, New Mexico, though they didn't get but pocket change according to the report I got. I heard all this secondhand from Laura Lee through letters had the ink stained with her tears. Broke my heart to hear about it. I went down there to visit with her and get the whole story just after I got word I was in a fix my own self. Cancer of the stomach," he said with a finality that was like letting his breath out.

"And that's where the real tough news came, when I got down that way."

I thought about Luz, my life here, how I'd pulled away from the violent life I'd once lived. I looked up at the gravesites of my friend Tom Twist, on the hill where I'd buried him, and the woman he'd loved and died over, both of them buried side by side now and forever together. I thought about the men I'd already killed and sometimes dreamed about—the dreams always bad, but what told me it was time to quit was when I stopped dreaming about them.

Then for a time I took to drinking hard and fell pretty low on the ladder of humanity.

I drifted for a year or so, mending fence and working for other men and getting into my own sorts of trouble with liquor and women. I got into fistfights because I was good with my fists and

I liked how it felt to beat a man down who gave me trouble, like it wasn't so much beating *him* down as it was the trouble that dogged me.

Then I woke up one morning from a hard drunk, lying face up on the high desert with rain in my face and my horse and saddle stole along with my boots. And if whoever it was hadn't also stole my guns, I do believe I would have killed myself then and there because I was a man past forty without a future and I knew I either had to lie there and die or get up and walk.

I was cold and miserable and hung over, and out of nowhere a dog came up and started licking my face, and something made me hug it because it was love I was most in need of, and I guess that old dog was looking for the same thing.

I asked the dog if it was Jesus come to save me and it barked and I said, "Well if you ain't, you're close enough." And I got up and started walking and the dog followed me and stayed with me for a time, then went off on its own soon as I got to within sights of the next town.

I hated to see that dog go, but I knew we all had to choose our own way and it had to choose its own way as well. That's just the way life is.

I ended up getting hired on as a deputy town marshal and tending bar in some broke dick Texas town that has since burned to the ground and never rebuilt as far as I know of. Then one day a telegram showed up for me from Dalton Stone, the father of the woman buried up on the hill next to my friend Tom Twist.

It said in effect he'd been trying to find me ever since that day I showed him her grave and told him the story of how she and Tom were hunted down by her abusive husband and was killed by him and some of his hired men, and how much he appreciated it that I, in turn, had killed the husband, Johnny Waco, and those same hired men. He'd wanted to do something for me then but I'd refused, because I didn't take pay for doing what was the right thing to do. He went on to say in the telegram the offer of money or whatever I needed was still standing and he'd like to hear from me and know what I was up to, that he'd feel forever indebted to me and would I please wire him back.

Well, I thought about it for a few days and counted what I had in my savings account— forty-four dollars and seventy-five cents—a dollar for every year I'd lived and change. I remembered there was this little place I'd seen for sale on the Rio Penasco that used to belong to Charlie Bowdre, who'd run with Billy the Kid until Garrett put a bullet in them both.

Charlie's place was a little run down but it had a good view of the river and the grass around it was sweet for grazing horses—a venture I thought I could do well at: catching and breaking wild horses and selling them. So I wired Mr. Stone back and thanked him and said if he wanted to do something, he might consider loaning me the money to buy the place and I'd pay him back as my horse venture grew.

That's how it came to pass that I'm in this place now, with horses in the corral and a woman who comes and cleans my house and has supper with me and stays the night once a week. I built a little porch on the front too. Now here was a sort of trouble I didn't need or want at my kitchen table.

"What is it you're asking of me, Cap'n?"

He leaned forward, setting his cup down, then stood and walked over to the window above the sink. He stared out for a long few moments, the sun on the glass now so that the frost was melted away.

Without turning to look at me, he said, "This is the part that's real bad, Jim. I have to kill one of them boys."

Chapter Three

I sat listening as the Cap'n explained it. All the time I'd known the Cap'n, I'd never known him to fail at anything he set his mind to, and I never saw him flinch from danger or falter under fire.

But now I noticed his body tremble as he spoke.

"What do you mean, Cap'n, say it plain."

He turned to face me then, his features drawn into a mask of sorrow.

"They made a big mistake, those grandsons of mine," he began. "They crossed the border into Old Mexico and something real bad happened—a woman got raped and killed, the daughter of a Ruales general. They caught Billy and Sam at the scene. Billy confessed it was his doing and none of Sam's. And the General would have probably let Sam ride but Billy broke out of jail, and he was the only one got away. Sam's still locked up down there in their calaboose. Billy made his way back across the border and wired his mother what happened, asking her to wire me and send a company of Rangers down there. I still got some contacts down there and found out who it was, this general. Just so happens I knew old Pancho Toro from back during my border days, back before he *was* a general or even a soldier.

"We worked the same cattle outfit together and used to drink and gamble together, both of us still green kids."

Cap'n shook his head, remembering.

"He was a hell of a vaquero is all I knew. We grew to be friends. He was even set to marry my sister Alice but she died of the influenza before they could tie the knot. After that we just sort of went our separate ways. Once I got word it was

29

Pancho holding Sam I wired him direct and explained to him who Sam was to me. He wired me back saying he had a lot of sympathy for me but if I wanted to save Sam's skin, I would have to track Billy down and kill him since he and his Ruales couldn't cross the river north and do it themselves . . ."

Then a great weight seemed to settle on the Cap'n's shoulders, for he visibly sagged.

"He says to prove I killed Billy I had to cut off his head and bring it to him or else he was going to execute Sam in Billy's stead. Said somebody had to pay, and if not Billy, then Sam. I don't doubt for a minute he'll do it. You know anything about Mexican men, you know they got a lot of pride in their manhood and are real macho types. Says I've got two weeks to get Billy killed. Not much more time than what the doctors tell me I got to live. So you can see I'm in a bit of a tight spot here, Jim."

Cap'n came back over to the table and sat down and said, "Maybe you could pour me another bit of that forty rod." And I filled the bottom of his cup with whiskey.

"You want me to find Billy and kill him for you, is that it?" I said.

His face knotted in pain.

"No sir. Not quite."

"Then what?"

"I'd just like you to go along with me in case

my own deal goes bad before I can see it done. You'd be my backup plan."

"You mean kill Billy in case you don't make it that long, then go get Sam from the General?"

"Yes sir. That's about the way of it. I can't save them both but if I can save one, it will be better than watching them both go down."

"And you think you can kill your own grandson, do it the way the General wants it done?" I said.

He looked at me level then, with a gaze I'd seen before.

"You know I've always been a man who does whatever needs doing," he said after taking another swallow of the whiskey. "Even if it is about to be the most terrible thing I've ever done."

"Can I ask you something?" I said.

"You've every right."

"How come you want me in on this and not one of your other men?"

"You were right on the way," he said.

"How come I don't believe that's the real reason?"

"You know that ain't it, but do I have to explain it?"

I shook my head. I knew what he meant: I was as bad as him when it came to killing men. How could I convince him I'd changed, that I'd met Luz and just the pure gentleness of a woman can change a man's heart and make him want more than what he's been used to all his life? Luz's love took all the fighting out of me, all the blood-letting ways I used to have.

His gaze continued to hold mine steady. There was one other reason I think he was asking me, even though he didn't say a word about it: the fact he'd saved my life once. But the Cap'n wasn't the sort of man to come right out and say he was calling in his marker.

"What if we can't find Billy in the time the General's given you and goes ahead and executes Sam?" I said.

"Then I aim to go down there and kill him, and if I ain't able, then I'm asking you go down and kill him for me. But I don't think it will come to all that, because I know where Billy is and how to get him."

I heard the stud whicker out in the corral. Cap'n looked up, and for a brief moment I saw light in his eyes. He was a pure horseman.

"Well, think about it at least," he said, standing and turning stiffly toward the door. "I'll be waiting for the afternoon flyer to Tucson. Billy's locked up in jail down near there. All I got to do is go on down there and take him out and . . ."

He opened the door, and the cold touched my skin like a piece of flatiron.

I walked him out to the hack and watched him struggle to get up and in. He sat there a minute catching his breath, looking off toward the horses.

"That big buckskin stud looks like he'd rip you

a new one," he said. "You tried to ride him yet?"

"Every day since I caught him. Keeps pitching me off and trying to stomp my brains out. Don't know why I just don't cut him loose and let him go on back to where he came from."

"Where'd he come from?"

I pointed.

"Way out yonder beyond those hills," I said. "I don't know why I wasted my time catching him in the first place. Should have known better."

"He'll make you a hell of a horse if you can get him rode."

"I don't know as he can be rode."

Cap'n looked at him for a long time, then said, "He can be rode, old son. Any horse can be rode, just like any cowboy can be throwed. It just takes the right man on the right horse to do it is all."

He snapped the reins and turned the hack back toward the road to Coffin Flats, and I stood watching him go and half wished he'd never come in the first place because I sure as hell hated to see a good man like him so busted down and sick and with such troubles to deal with in his last days.

There was snow on the mountains that would be there all winter no matter how warm it might get down here in the valley. I turned to walk back to the house when my gaze swept the ridge where Tom and Antonia are buried, their headstones with a cap of snow on them.

I walked on up there. It was a bit of a climb.

33

The wind was blowing up from the south now, bringing some warmth.

"Got me a problem," I said when I reached the graves, kneeling in front of Tom's. Tom was always a good listener. "Cap'n wants me to go help him kill his grandson, just a kid, really, nineteen, but old enough, I reckon, to pay for his crimes. I don't want to do it. I like it right here just fine. Me and you and Luz and this old place and them horses is about all I ever wanted and all I'll ever need."

Way off down in the valley the other side of the river, I could see a lone coyote loping along, its rough, rusty fur catching the sun.

I brushed aside some of the snow on the ground and picked up a handful of pebbles.

"I don't want to do no more killing either," I said. "I go do this thing, I'm right back where I said I'd never go again."

A gust of wind brushed along the ground.

"And I still got that damn stud to ride so I can get him gentle enough to be bred up with those mares and maybe sell him to a rich man. I got lots of damn things to do right here without running off to Arizona or Old Mexico, or some such."

I watched the coyote come down to the river's edge, look back the direction from which it had come, then straddle and drink.

"What would you do were you me?" I said.

Tom had been a chaplain's assistant in the

Union Army and later a preacher before his wife died and he began to drift in search of answers to questions he said pressed on him after her death. And by the time I'd met him, he said he hadn't found any answers yet. All I could hope was he found them in that last hour of his life, or he'd found them when he crossed over from this world to the next.

"You're not going to tell me, are you?" I said.

The coyote loped off upriver like something was chasing him but he wasn't scared.

I shook the pebbles in my hand like dice.

"Why the hell did you have to go and die on me?" I said. Another gust of wind caught in my shirt.

I stood and walked back down to the house, but instead of going inside, I went to the shed and got my saddle, then walked to the small corral I had the stud in.

I slung the saddle on the top rail.

The stud eyed me like he knew the jig was up for one of us.

"Today's the day," I said. "I'm feeling like a dance."

He whinnied and tossed his head.

"You're going to get rode or I'm going to get throwed, but this is the last day we do this thing if it ain't one or the other."

He was a block of muscle and fury, a cyclone of a horse the color of the desert, with a line running down his back, black as death. Just standing there looking at him reminded me I still had plenty of bruises from the last several times I'd tried to break him.

I crawled between the lower rails and took my rope and let out a loop. There was no place for him to run except along the back rails. I tossed my rope and let it fall over his head, then wrapped it twice around the snubbing post, and he kicked and screamed like a banker who was being robbed.

"You can raise all the damn hell you want," I said. I waited till he settled into a stiff-legged stand.

Sometimes you fail at something and you can't understand why you did. You figure you gave it all you had and it still didn't work out and you're ready to quit it all, figuring you got nothing left to give. Then something makes you try one last time. And this time you dig down deep into a place you never even knew was there, just an extra inch more, an extra ounce of strength. Your mind locks down tight on the thing you're determined to do—and suddenly it's just enough to get it done.

So I got my blanket and saddle on him and my bit in his teeth and swung aboard. The first few seconds forked on the stud was like riding a runaway freight train that had crashed off a gorge into a rocky canyon bottom. I thought he was going to snap my head off and pull both arms out of the sockets. But when he hadn't thrown me on the first several tries, I got into a rhythm with him, and it was like dancing with a crazy woman. Only I felt even crazier this time. Whatever move the stud made I anticipated. It was like I suddenly was part of him and he was part of me.

He kicked down the rails and busted down the gate. He snorted and stomped and kicked and bucked all over what you might call a yard, and then suddenly there went my chicken fence and coop—those hens and that rooster scattering like ten sorts of hell was after them, the coop busted to boards. The stud was just a damn cyclone but I stuck and finally rode him down.

And then he just stood there under me, blowing hard, his whole body quivering, and I waited for him to make another go at it but when he didn't, I touched my heels to his sides and walked him around with that Spanish bit in his mouth, and he learned fast what it was there for. I stroked his powerful sweaty neck and walked him over to the water and let him take a drink, then rode him all the way to the ridge and showed him off to Tom and Antonia. And for a time we just sat there with the wind in our faces. Then I rode him back down and the stud did everything I asked of him, though he still had a lot of strut to him, but that was okay—it was the way I wanted him.

I had myself a good horse.

And an old man who needed my help.

I went inside and packed a bedroll with a few

extra clothes in it: shirts, socks, pair of jeans. Packed my saddlebags with razor, soap, comb, two boxes of shells for the Merwin Hulbert that was in my bottom dresser drawer, pocket knife, general things I'd need. I went and got my pistol and unwrapped it from the towel and slid it into the shoulder rig, then strapped it on before putting on my coat. I took the Henry rifle from the corner by the door and slipped it into a scabbard and walked outside again and rigged everything to the saddle. I looked around at my wrecked yard and thought I should probably try and round up those damn chickens and that rooster, but decided against it. You can always buy more chickens and a rooster.

I rode to Gin Walker's place halfway between my place and town and stopped and asked him if he'd look after my stock—that I'd be gone a few weeks, maybe longer. I knew he'd do it because that's what neighbors do for each other. He said no problem, and I could see him eyeing the brass butt of the Henry sticking out of the scabbard and probably wondering what I was up to, but he didn't say anything.

I thanked him and headed for town.

It was a pretty day.

I figured I'd better stop and tell Luz I'd be gone for a time. It seemed only fair.

I just hoped that, unlike the chickens, she'd be there when I returned.

Chapter Four

He was sitting there in front of the station, in the shade of the eaves on a wood bench smoking a cigarette. He was leaned forward with his forearms resting on the thighs of his faded jeans, his mackinaw unbuttoned and hanging loose. The sun had come up and melted most of the snow that had fallen through the night, and now the streets and roads were just a reddish mud the horses and wagons slopped through as they passed up and down. Women held their skirts up above the tops of their shoes as they walked wherever there weren't boards to walk on, and dogs stood grizzled with muddied legs, looking forlorn.

I rode up and stopped in front of the station, and he looked up and I could see just the merest recognition on his face and a sign of relief that I'd come. He looked at the stud and said, "I see you got him broke."

"Not without some disagreement," I said.

"You going to haul him along?"

"That's the plan. What about you?" I said. "What you going to do for a horse once we get down to Tucson?"

He drew on his cigarette and exhaled a cloud of

smoke, his fingers stained yellow from years of tobacco use.

"I'm going to rent a hack," he said. "Can't sit a horse no more. This burg they got Billy in is about fifty or so miles southwest of there, a place called Finger Bone. Train don't go there."

Stacked there beside him next to the bench was a small trunk and a Winchester rifle. He saw me glance at it.

"How'd you learn of him being in jail down there, Cap'n?"

Cap'n leaned his head forward and spit between his boots.

"Like I said, I got friends all over the Southwest."

I dismounted and went in and bought myself a ticket and stuck it in my shirt pocket, then came out and unsaddled the stud, and set the saddle along with my bedroll and kit there next to his things, and my rifle still in its scabbard next to his, and he looked at it and said, "I see you still favor the Henry rifle."

"It was good enough for me in Texas," I said. "I guess it's good enough for me here in New Mexico."

He drew on the smoke and shucked the nub into the muddy street, where it fizzled, and said, "I reckon so."

I glanced at my pocket watch, and there was still half an hour before the train was set to come in.

"I need to go do something," I said.

"Go ahead," he said. "I'll watch over your gear."

I went up the street toward Luz's place—a small adobe at the edge of town that had an ocotillo fence around it. She was there in the side yard hanging clothes from a wire line, white blouses and black and red skirts.

She turned when she heard me open the gate.

"Didn't think I'd see you again so soon," she said.

"I've come to tell you I'll be gone for a little while," I said.

The smile faded from her face as she brushed some loose strands of hair away from her forehead with the back of her wrist, a wet piece of clothing clutched in her hands.

"I thought you liked it here," she said. "Did you just say the other night how you didn't think you were ever going to leave here again?"

"Like it here more than anyplace else I've ever been."

"Then why go?"

"No choice."

She looked beyond me as if someone was standing behind me.

"We can choose to stay or we can choose to go," she said. "If you're going, it's because you choose to go, because you want to go, not because you have no choice."

I came up close to her. She was wearing a long-sleeved blouse and I could see the heaviness of

41

her breasts loose inside, and I wanted to take them in my hands through the cloth and hold them and feel their firm softness once more. Something dark and troubling had been working at me ever since I first saw the Cap'n's buggy black against the snow.

"It's because of that man that came to your house, isn't it?" she said.

"Yes."

She crossed herself as if she'd just stepped into the little church at the other end of the street—the one by the plaza where bailes were held every Saturday night if the weather was decent—and had a bell in the tower that would ring in the believers. An old padre with one good eye preached there, and some claimed he could perform miracles.

"I knew it," she whispered.

"He needs my help," I said. "I owe him from the past."

"What do you owe him?"

"My life."

"And now he wants it back."

"No. Not if I can help it."

She shrugged in resignation, shook loose a wet skirt she'd been holding, and hung it on the line.

"It's none of my business what you do," she said. "When and where you go and come. I'm just the woman who cleans your house."

"And sleeps in my bed," I said.

"Yes, and sleeps in your bed."

"I just wanted you to know," I said. "I figured I owed it to you to tell you."

"And now you have told me."

"Yes."

I turned to leave. She called my name.

"Jim."

I turned back, and she came close to me and pressed the palms of her hands against my chest.

"I'm afraid for you," she said. "I'm afraid you will go away and I will never see you again."

"You don't have to worry; there's nothing to this. I'm just going to ride along with the Cap'n while he does some business. You were right about him looking sick. He is. He's dying and is worried he won't get his business done before he passes on."

"What sort of business needs you wearing this?" she said, patting the bulge under my left armpit.

"You know how it is out here in this country," I said.

"Yes, I know how it is."

"I best get on," I said.

"I'll wait for you until the spring," she said. "After that I'll stop waiting for you." I wanted to laugh at her foolishness.

"I shouldn't be more than a couple of weeks at the outside."

"Do you want me to go and feed and water your horses?"

"No, I've asked Gin to do it."

"What about the chickens, should I go collect the eggs?"

"They're scattered all over hell," I said. "I broke the stud earlier and he kicked down the coop and fence and everything. I reckon those chickens could be in Colorado by now."

She smiled. I kissed her, then walked back up the street to the station.

Cap'n looked up when I approached like he knew something.

"You let her know you're going off?"

"Yes."

"You think you might end up marrying her?"

"It's possible."

"She strikes me as a good woman besides being real easy on a man's eyes. Women like that are hard to come by way out here in this frontier. Even no-account ugly women are hard to come by, but especially the real good-looking ones."

"There's more women than you might imagine if you like the Mexican kind," I said.

"I got nothing at all against Mexican women," he said. "They work hard and laugh a lot from what I know of them. I imagine yours does too."

I reached inside my coat pocket and took out the pint bottle of forty rod and handed it to him because he looked like he could stand a drink, and I sure as hell knew I could.

He looked at it before taking hold of it and

44

pulling the cork, then he put it to his mouth and swallowed. Then he looked at it again and handed it back to me, and I took a pull and plugged it and put it back inside my coat pocket.

"Sun's pretty on the snow on them mountains yonder," he said.

"It is, ain't it."

Way off in the distance we heard the train whistle blowing.

"She's coming," he said.

I pulled my watch and checked the time.

"Way early," I said.

"Lucky we're here then or we'd of missed it," he said.

"Ain't we though."

He stood slowly as though he had to fit everything into place, all his bones, before he could move properly.

"You don't owe me nothing," he said. "I don't want you to go on you thinking you owe me because of what happened that time in Caddo."

"I'm not thinking nothing like that."

He stared hard at me then.

" 'Cause if that's the case, I don't want you helping me. I don't operate like that, figuring a man owes me anything because of the past."

"Look, maybe it is some of that, but so what? You saved my skin in Caddo and if it wasn't for you killing those two bandits, I'd have been planted and no chance to help nobody or eat a nice

45

breakfast this morning or spend my nights with a good woman. So maybe it is a little of my thinking I owe you for something. But it's not just that."

"What is it then?"

The whistle grew louder, and you could see the black smoke of its engine chuffing into the air off in the distance like a small dark cloud.

"I guess you already know."

He nodded.

"I always just did my job, Jim, keeping you boys alive, you and the others. I didn't always, that's a natural fact, but I did the best I could because it was my job, that's all."

I couldn't say I thought of him like he was my own daddy, which he'd just about had been when I first joined the Rangers. I couldn't tell him that, nor would he have wanted me to. Men like him and me don't talk about such intimate things, but it didn't mean we didn't feel them.

"You did more than your job, Cap'n, a lot more."

He looked off again up the tracks.

"Here she comes," he said.

I held the reins to the stud. He was jumpy at the sight and noise his iron brother was making. I stroked his muzzle and spoke to him gentle. "Don't raise no fuss and make us have to go through what we did earlier all over again," I said. The stud tossed his head and whinnied.

"Maybe we ought to have another sip of old

Mr. Fortifier," Cap'n said. "Before we get on that train. Maybe you ought to give that half-broke horse a swally too so he won't kick out the sides of his car when they put him aboard."

I took out the bottle and handed it to the Cap'n, and he bit off a piece and handed it back.

"I used to be a teetotaler when I was married up with JoAnn. She was a righteous woman and wouldn't let me keep none in the house, and so I just gave it up along with every other wickedness when I got with her. She got me to being baptized standing waist deep in the Canadian River by a tongue-speaking preacher. She cleaned me up pretty good from what I had been. But I never claimed not to miss a good glass of whiskey or a good smoke, and now I just look at it as the best medicine a man can get himself."

"You don't need to explain nothing to me," I said.

"I know I don't."

Then we stood there waiting for the train to shudder to a stop.

Chapter Five

The Cap'n slept on and off as the train rolled through countryside that was mostly tan hills shaped like the crowns of sombreros, and laced with ocotillo that glittered in the sun like the white of an old man's hair. The red country turned to brown and the creek beds and washes we crossed were mostly dry, strewn with rocks and boulders—here and there thin streams of water laced down through the sandy draws.

Once I saw a herd of antelope way off in the distance grazing contently, their tails swishing the flies.

The Cap'n would wake every now and then and say, "Where are we, Jim?" And I would guess and he'd nod and then close his eyes again, and I thought, *You must be plum wore out, Gus, go ahead and sleep in peace while you can.*

His coat was parted open and I saw the familiar pearl grips of his Smith & Wesson Russian model—something he'd always carried ever since I've known him. It was a .44 caliber that had seen its fair share of work. I knew because I'd seen it in action up close and personal on more than one occasion. The Cap'n was a dead shot even under fire. I asked him about that, how he never missed.

He said, "You just can't think about it, you just aim and shoot what you're aiming at. You start thinking, you're probably going to hesitate, and that can be a fatal mistake in a gunfight." He proved his point that time in Caddo when we ran this half-breed gang to ground. We'd been dogging their trail for weeks over some robberies and killings they had committed in the Panhandle. Our party of Rangers took them on in a last stand they'd made there in that little town, and we killed five of them and they two of us.

We thought we'd killed them all, and while the Cap'n went to send a wire to our headquarters in Fort Griffen that the Juarez Gang was no longer, the rest of our party licked its wounds and set about burying our dead. Then when that was complete, we allowed as to how we needed to rest our horses a day or so before starting home. I took the opportunity to go into the town and get myself a haircut and shave.

It was while I was there in the barber's chair with a hot towel on my face I felt something small and hard suddenly pressed against my temple and the stink of bad breath. I heard the hammer of a pistol being thumbed back, accompanied by a rough Spanish voice saying, "*Señor, usted mata a algunos de nosotros, nosotros mata a alga de usted, eh?*"

I'd learned enough Spanish to understand he was telling me it was my turn to die, to more or less even the score for the ones we'd killed of his. I peeked up through the towel and saw it was old Vaca Juarez—a half Apache, half Mexican—himself standing there, short and heavyset like a man who ate too much beans and fried bread. With him was a rough-looking character of about the same stumpy stature, holding a Walker Colt the size of a small cannon. Cross-eyed little bastard with a wispy mustache and whiskers looked like they were made out of black silk threads sewn into his upper lip and chin.

I eased the towel from my face and saw the barber standing there holding his straight razor down along his leg, looking about as fearful as I was beginning to feel. You always think you're ready to die when the time comes. But the simple truth is, you never are when it actually comes. You could be eighty years old and bullet shot and still not ready. I was still relatively young at forty-five and in pretty good health, and sure as hell not ready to cash in my hand.

I saw the bottles of shave lotion and talc sitting on the shelf in front of the mirror, saw my reflection and that of the three men standing—the barber and the two bandits holding their pistols on me and every right to be pissed off, because we'd flat laid out their companions in the earlier fight like planks, side by side, so the local newspaperman could take photographs of them before we buried them in a hasty common grave.

The sour smell of the bandits mixed with the talcum powder and shave lotions on the barber's shelf. I saw patches of hair that had been cut from my head lying there on the floor, and thought that dying in a barber's chair was about the last place I'd have guessed I was going to fold my hand if somebody had asked me. But it sure as hell looked that way, and I just hoped old Vaca had a good aim and generous heart and finished me with one bullet and not two or three. Sometimes a man wanted to make you suffer before he finished you off; he shot you in the knees or through the hands, just to make you suffer awhile.

I waited for the bullet that would kill me, knowing I'd never even hear the shot. I closed my eyes because I didn't want to see it. But then I did hear a shot that caused me to flinch. And when I opened my eyes, the man holding the pistol to my head fell like a stone dropped down a well at the same instant his blood and brains splattered across my unshaven face. The Mexican with him yelled something I couldn't make out, a bastardized cussword. But before he could get the word all the way out of his mouth the Cap'n shot him too, dead center of his forehead. The bullet bucked him back and he crashed to the floor and lay there next to old Vaca, who had a ribbon of blood coming from underneath his head.

51

I swiped the bloody offal from my face as I saw the Cap'n standing there, his gun still held straight out, smoke curling from the muzzle before he slowly lowered it and slipped it into his holster.

"You okay?" he said that day.

"I'm not sure, but I don't hurt nowhere."

He took his bandana from round his neck and dipped it in a pan of water the barber used to wash off his razor, and handed it to me, saying, "Warsh your face, Jim. Get that stinking bandit's blood off you."

He never once mentioned how I should have been more careful, or lectured me about making the mistake of letting the bandits get the cold drop on me. He just shot those two like they were quail, then put his gun away, waiting for me to wash my face. I'd always wanted to talk to him about it, about what it felt like to be so near being murdered, because a thing like that sticks with you worse than your worst dreams. I wanted to just talk about it after I'd had time to get my wits about me, but I knew he wasn't the type to discuss such matters—that life was just what it was; you either lived or you died and that was the end of it. Didn't matter how close you might *have* come to dying. Life for him at least was like a game of horseshoes—*close didn't count.* And if it didn't count, then why talk about it?

But I figured I owed him my life even if he didn't.

● ● ●

I saw a sign the following day out the window
that read: NOW ENTERING ARIZONA TERRITORY.
And when the Cap'n woke up from napping, I told
him we'd crossed the border and he nodded and
said, "Well, it don't look no different, does it?"

"No sir, it don't." Then he closed his eyes again
and I walked out to the platform of the caboose.

A black porter was standing there smoking. He
started to strip away his shuck but I waved him
not to.

"Don't need to put it out on my account," I said.

"Yas suh."

The clatter of the train's steel wheels against the
track rose and fell with an easy steady rhythm.
The porter said, "Nothing like train music."

"You like working on the railroad," I said.

"Beats lots of other things," he said. He was
middle-aged with very black skin, and wore a
black jacket and wrinkled trousers that were a
few inches too short and a pair of rough brown
brogans.

He reached in his pocket and took out his
makings and extended them to me, and I thanked
him and rolled myself a shuck, then handed his
makings back. He handed me a match, and I
struck it off the side of the car and cupped the
flame in my hands to light my smoke, then
snapped out the match and flipped it away. I never
smoked before I met Luz. She's the one got me

into the habit, just watching her smoke there in the evenings out on the porch of my place after supper. I liked the smell of it and I had her roll me a shuck, and after the first few draws I got used to it. She's the only woman I ever knew who smoked cigarettes and looked good doing it.

The porter and me stood there smoking with the rocking of the car beneath our feet, not saying anything because we were of two different worlds, the porter and I, but maybe not so different than a lot of people might think. I'm sure, like me, the man had seen his share of troubles and heartache. And I'm sure, like me, all he mostly wanted was a decent life, a steady job, and to live in peace.

"You like horses?" I said.

He smiled broadly.

"I used to ride 'em in the army," he said. "I was a buffalo soldier with the Ninth. Fought the Comanche, the Apache and Kiowa too. All over Texas mostly." He had a wistfulness about it when he spoke of it. He took off his cap and rubbed his shaved head.

"The Indians gave us the name because they said our hair reminded them of the buffaloes. I always kept mine shaved because I figured if they ever killed me I didn't want them to hang my scalp from their belts." The corners of his eyes crinkled when he smiled.

"We got that in common," I said, thinking aloud

about how in my early years as a Ranger we fought some of those same peoples at places like Adobe Walls and Palo Duro Canyon.

"Huh?" he said.

"Nothing," I said. "Just talking to myself."

"It ain't no problem," he said. "I best get back on inside."

I nodded and watched him take one last precious draw from his shuck, then grind it down under his shoe heel.

Light lay along the twin ribbons of steel tracks that ran like two thin rivers behind the train. The smell of hot cinder rose from the track bed as a black erratic cloud of engine smoke floated lazily overhead. I thought of the thousands of Chinese that laid these tracks in their cotton pajamas and coolie hats, their backs bent to the task, how they must have squatted in the shade of their own making for lunch and the few daily breaks from the onerous work and chatted in their own language about their faraway homeland, wondering no doubt if they'd made a mistake coming here to this wild and endless frontier. I guess in some ways they were like that black porter; designated to their lot in life by the color of their skin and nothing else. Just men trying to make it from one day to the next while waiting for something impossible to happen that would change their circumstances, like a man who waits for love or money or God.

I went back in and sat across from the Cap'n. A woman in a dark blue gingham dress sat across the aisle from us reading a small book with red leather covers, her feathered hat resting on the empty seat beside her. She glanced up when I came and took my seat, and our eyes met, and she smiled and I returned the smile, then she returned to reading.

We rode on through the day and into evening, into the darkening land that lay ahead of us and descended behind us. We rode on like two errant knights off to slay the dragon—only the dragon was a kid named Billy, son of the Cap'n's daughter who always made poor choices when it came to men.

Chapter Six

We stepped off the train in Tucson at around noon the following day. It looked ramshackle, like a bandito hideout. Up the street a group of men were gathered watching a cockfight. Two oily red roosters with steel spurs were tearing into each other, and I don't know who was squawking more, those chickens or the men betting on them.

Cap'n shook his head and said, "What men won't bet on."

He spat in the dust.

"What's our next move?" I said.

"We go and rent me a hack and drive to Finger Bone."

"You know how to get there?"

"No, but I can ask."

I unloaded my stud and saddled him, and tied on my rifle in its scabbard and bedroll behind the cantle. Cap'n carried his Winchester in one hand and his valise in the other. The sun scorched the dusty street so that when we walked our footsteps raised little puffs of brown dust that settled over the toes of our boots, and we got as far as a saloon that simply had the word SALOON painted in black on the adobe facing over the wood door.

"Maybe we ought to stop and get us a cold beer and something to eat," he said. "I'll bet you're hungry." We hadn't eaten anything since yesterday. We went inside and found a table, and the waiter came over and we ordered a couple of ice beers, and the Cap'n said, "Can you read that menu?" It was a chalkboard above the bar and featured beef stew and sausages and cabbage. I read it aloud and he said he'd try his hand at the sausages and cabbage. I ordered the stew. The Cap'n only nibbled at his food.

"It ain't setting too well with me, Jim. Not much is these days." Then he motioned the waiter over and asked if he had any bread and milk, and the waiter said he thought he had but he'd have to check the ice house. Then soon enough he came back with a saucer of milk and a loaf of crusty bread, and this the Cap'n tore off in small chunks and dipped into the milk and ate fairly well for a man in his condition. I could only imagine what that was like—to have cancer in your stomach.

We mostly ate in silence. Finally the Cap'n had enough and ordered us each a glass of whiskey.

"Finger Bone's where you said they got Billy locked up?" I commented as I washed down the last of the food with what was left in my beer glass before tossing back the shot of rye.

"Yes sir." Then he proceeded to tell me about Ira Hayes, the local lawman in Finger Bone, how Ira used to be a cattle and horse rustler and real hard drinker till the Cap'n caught up with him in a whorehouse after dogging him for the better part of a month.

"Ira at that time was living with a three-hundred-pound whore and selling snakehead whiskey to the savages down in the Oklahoma panhandle. The marshals were after him as well, but I caught him first. I come up on him taking a siesta, his big feet sticking off the end of the bed. The son of a buck was well over six and a half feet tall. His big gal jumped on me like I was a pony at the fair and tried to bash my head in with her fists. I had to lay her out, Jim. I swear I'm not about hitting women, but this one was about to ride me under. Then I called for him to surrender. Which he did quite well. He asked me right off as I was putting the manacles on him if I was a God-fearing man, was I in the Good Book regular, and I said I was, and even if I hadn't been, just looking around that den of iniquity of a town, where the saloons maintained a noticeable predominance over every other sort of dwelling, I'd sure enough become a righteous man from thinking I'd just landed in hell itself . . . Then I asked him why he wanted to know and he said because he'd been having thoughts lately about turning his life around . . ."

The Cap'n again displayed a rare smile in the telling of how he first met Ira Hayes.

"He wore two guns, real rare," the Cap'n said. "But one had a busted hammer and the other had busted grips, and when I relieved him of them and made commentary on his poor firearms, he laughed and said, 'Hell, I ain't a killing man nohow. Onliest way I'd kill a feller with my guns was if one went off accidental, or I was to throw one at him and it somehow knocked his brains out.' I said, 'Well, you are under arrest for horse thieving and cattle rustling and that's that.' He asked me would I pray with him and help show him the way to the Lord. I said, 'Right here, you mean?' His whore was laid out like a Belgium carpet there on the floor where I knocked her, and it was such a bad place you could taste the sin in the air. 'Yes sir,' says he, 'right here and right now, for I am sick to death of my criminal ways and want the good Lord to take mercy on me like he did them sinners on the hill.' So we prayed and I felt a change in him and promised if he ever needed anything when he got out of the jailhouse to let me know. Didn't hear from him for several years, then one day I got a letter from him telling me he was doing all right for himself, going to church regular, and wanted to know if I'd write a letter of recommendation for this lawman's job in Finger Bone—said he had a wife and a new child on the way and could use regular work. I wrote the letter and sent it to him and he wired me back later and said he'd got the job. That was three years ago."

It was the most I'd ever heard the Cap'n say at one time. I wondered if he'd gotten windy knowing his time was short, and everything he needed to get said, he needed to get said before it got too late. He swallowed down the whiskey the Mexican brought to the table, and it allowed some color back in his sallow cheeks.

"So the second stroke of luck, if you can call it that, was it was Ira who arrested Billy for trying to steal a horse, and Billy ended up confessing to him the whole sad story about what happened down in Old Mexico and that he'd wired his ma to try and get me to come down with my Rangers, and that's how it come out about who Billy was to me. Ira right quick sent me a telegram. I wired him back and said, 'Hold him till I get there.' "

"You tell Ira what's going to happen once you get Billy?"

"No sir. That's between us."

I saw how the thought of it drew down the corners of Cap'n's eyes and mouth into something grim and weary. He swiped whiskey dew off his mustaches with a forefinger and stood and took a moment to straighten himself, leaning his weight on the back of his chair but acting like it was a natural act and not something born of his pain.

"We best go rent that hack," he said. On the way out he asked the waiter where there was a stable, and the man told him and we went up the street past the cockfight where the dead roosters lay in a pile of bloody feathers, their owners having twisted off their heads and fed them to several stray cats lurking about.

Cap'n said, "I guess a man takes his pleasure where he can find it," as we walked past the knot of shouting men. "I personally don't see no sport in killing chickens."

A caballero sitting under a big straw hat with some of the crown eat out probably by rats was dozing on a three-legged stool in front of the barn. You could smell the sweet scent of hay and horseshit lingering in the heat.

The man's arms hung straight down from his sides like he'd been shot dead, only hadn't yet fallen over. Cap'n kicked him lightly on the sole of his huaraches, and he woke with a start, pushing back the flop brim of his sombrero.

"Sí!"

Cap'n told him in Spanish he'd come to rent a hack, and they haggled the price because it was a common thing to do, haggling. Most of these birds felt slighted if you didn't haggle with them. They came to terms in short order because the Cap'n was by nature an impatient man. The caballero went and hitched a horse to a hack, and the Cap'n paid him in silver. Then the Cap'n pointed and said, "That the road to Finger Bone?" The caballero nodded.

"Sí."

"You're a fellow of few words, ain't you?" Cap'n said.

The caballero shrugged, not understanding the joke.

I mounted my horse and rode alongside the hack at an easy pace.

"We should get there by nightfall," he said.

And I couldn't help but think that by morning, Billy would be dead and the old man would feel worse than he ever felt in his entire life, and I probably would as well, just having to witness it.

Chapter Seven

In the dying heat you could smell the grease-wood. The horses stepped along, raising dust to their fetlocks, their tongues fighting the bit.

"You doing okay?" I said.

The Cap'n kept a steady eye on the road in front of him. Off to the north a distant ridge of gray mountains seemed to shimmer in the haze.

Suddenly his horse shied in its traces and he fought it down while I shot the rattler that had crawled out onto the road, the Cap'n saying, "Snakes and horses just don't mix and never will." He skirted his rig around the carcass because the horse wouldn't have none of it. The damn thing was long as a man's leg and thick through the body as your wrist.

"Everything bites, stings, or sticks you in this country," he said. "They even got what they call jumping cactus out here—cholla, they call it." Then he grimaced in pain from something obviously troubling him on the inside, and his face was bathed in sweat, his color ashen.

I spotted a lone cabin off the road to our right, up a trace that cut through the desert.

"Why don't we pull off and see can we

water the horses at that house yonder," I said.

"Lead the way," he said without debating me on it.

The house set back about a quarter of a mile and the trace was rutted with deep wheel tracks that had cut through the earth when it was wet from the rainy season and baked hard again with the sun, and each time the Cap'n's wheels caught and jiggled the hack, his face took on the look of a man being punched in the gut.

We got within calling distance of the house—a combination of mud and wood with a tin roof run through with rust streaks, a small stone chimney at one end and a by-God gazebo in the yard. Off to the right was a couple of lean-tos, a wagon with the tongue laid on the ground. Farther on was a privy. Off to the left rear stood a pile of rusting cans.

I called the house.

Old man stepped out with a big bore in his hands down below his waist, not aiming but ready to use it if he had to.

"What you fellers want?" he said cautiously.

"Wanted to know if we could water our horses," I said.

He looked from me to the Cap'n.

"Don't figger you're trouble," he said. "Never known killers and troublemakers to go around in a hack. Water trough is out back."

"You mind I step down and stretch my legs and

maybe use that privy of yours?" the Cap'n said.

The old man nodded.

"Hep yourself," he said.

I led the horses around back to the water trough and let them drink while the Cap'n trudged off to the outhouse, then pretty soon trudged back again. I heard him in there retching. Then I walked the horse back round to the front where the Cap'n now sat making palaver with the old man there in the shade of a partial roof of what could be considered the start of a porch, but I'd never bet it was going to get finished anytime soon, if ever.

"How you making it way out here?" Cap'n was asking the old man. Well, I say old, but truth be told, the old man was probably the same age as the Cap'n, just more gnarled, like a wind-twisted tree trunk.

"Making do as best I can," the old man replied. "I come out here in '50, back when it was still wild and overrun with Chirichua and Lipan Apaches. Met old Geronimo and Natchez and their bands right here, near my well yonder. We palavered some and I think they would have cut my head off and put it on a pike, except I was married to an Apache woman at the time and she spoke up for me, saying how I was a good man and friend to the Induns, and they said long as I was married to her I didn't have nothing to worry about from them. That son of a bitch Geronimo had eyes like candle flames."

"That so," the Cap'n said. The old man nodded.

"You want a drink? I got some peddler's whiskey in the house I could abuse you boys with."

"Yes sir, we sure could use a drink of something stronger than well water," the Cap'n said.

"You look as if you could. Wait here, I'll go in and get the jug."

Cap'n looked at me and nodded.

"You learn to talk to folks right, you can get along pretty well in this old life," he said.

I looked off to where the sun was edging down behind some low brown hills, the rays of its light glancing upward and outward like the earth was catching fire.

"I bet that old boy has seen some things in his times," the Cap'n said. "I heard Geronimo was a real bad actor. Heard they put him in a jail down in Florida, Natchez too and their whole band."

"I bet he knows he's a lucky man to still be living," I said.

The old man came out, said, "My name's Torvor, Waylon Torvor, 'case you was interested," and handed Cap'n a brown glazed crock jug. The Cap'n took it up by the handle and hitched its bulk over his shoulder and tipped the neck to his mouth for a good long pull, then swung it over to the old man, who held it out to me. I stepped forward, and he grinned a dark brown–toothed grin through the grizzle of his maw and said, "You ain't Mormons, are you?"

"No sir, we ain't. What makes you think we are?"

"Nothing," the old man said.

I took a pull and was surprised how top-notch the liquor was. I handed it back and he took a pull and said, "Goddamn," and did a hitch step.

"You want another?" he said to the Cap'n.

"No sir, we got several miles yet to go and I'd not want to fall out of that hack and break my neck along that there lonely road and have to be buried so far from my home."

"Where you hail from?"

"Texas," is all the Cap'n would say.

"Texas," the old man said, like he was tasting the word. "Now that's a goddamn place and a half, it sure is. I once got married in Texas to a six-foot-tall whore—this was before I married the Apache woman, of course—who outweighed me by thirty pounds. This was in my wild youth. They grow everything big in Texas including their women." He cackled and snapped the jug up to his mouth again, happy for a reason to drink and palaver. And when he finished, he wiped off his mouth with the frayed cuff of his shirt sleeve.

"I buy my liquor off a whiskey drummer comes through here in the spring and fall. Says he has it shipped in from Kentucky. It fortifies me against all illnesses and dark times."

"Yes sir," the Cap'n said, trying to be polite. He wasn't a man to carry on an overlengthy conversation, nor listen to one either. He edged away from under the overhang and stepped toward his hack, and I could see it took every ounce of his strength to make it that far.

The old man called, "You boys is welcome to stay the night. Can camp out there in that shed if you like. Don't make nothing to me if you do. Got water and feed for your hosses. Just charge you a dollar for the feed. Good straw in that shed to make you a bed."

Cap'n looked at me.

"What do you think?" he said. The sky overhead had turned the color of sheet iron now that the sun had nearly gone out of it.

"How far is it to Finger Bone?" I asked the old man.

"Oh, I'd say another twelve, fifteen miles, but you daren't get caught out on that road after dark—too many highwaymen. They catch you out on that road, just the two of you, they'll set on you like chickens on a june bug. Real bad fellers patrol that road at night."

"I'm about tuckered out, Jim," the Cap'n said.

"You want us to bed down here for the night, that's okay with me," I said.

He looked off toward the dimming sky.

"It'll be dark before we got another two miles," he said. "I don't guess it'd make no difference if we get there late tonight or first thing in the morning."

I couldn't tell if his reluctance to push on was due to his feeling poorly or just that he knew what lay ahead of him, what he had to do once he got there.

"Maybe we ought to give it a rest then," I said.

He nodded.

The old man said, "I got a pot of beans with some fatback cooking in the firebox. We can all sit down to eat whenever you're ready."

I walked over and paid him the money for the horses' feed and then turned both animals out into the small corral he had there with his bunch of nags. I grained them down, then went and washed my hands and face at the pump and wiped off with my bandana.

The Cap'n was seated on one of the chairs the old man carried out from inside and set in the front of the house. The last of the sun was just then winking out beyond the smoke gray mountains off to the west. A soft dying wind ruffled the Cap'n's striped shirt. I sat on the edge of the porch.

"You thinking about tomorrow, when we get to Finger Bone and get your grandson?" I said.

"I am, can't help but to think about it."

"I'll do it for you if you want," I said. "I'll take care of that business for you."

He looked at me with troubled eyes.

"I couldn't ask that of you."

"You don't have to ask it."

"Shit," he said. It was one of the few times I'd ever heard him swear.

"You think about it," I said. "It's no skin off my neck you want me to do it."

"You think you could, just shoot a man like that?" he said. "A kid who never did a thing to you and wasn't trying to kill you back?"

"Put a gun in his hand if it will make you feel better."

He grunted.

"Ain't me that would need feeling better if *you* was to do it."

"It wouldn't make me feel better either way."

"I keep wondering what would get into him so bad, make him do something like what he done to that woman."

I shrugged and took out my makings and rolled myself a shuck, and it made me think of being out in the evening after supper with Luz, the two of us smoking and sipping liquor and talking.

"I sure wish I had a cold pear," the Cap'n said suddenly, sipping another bit of the peddler whiskey. "I do admire cold pears. Ever since I got told what I had by the physician, I'll get a craving for something now and then. The sweet kind you get in a can with the syrup in it."

I knew he wanted to change the subject, and I did too. I'd kill the kid if he wanted me to. I'd do it to save him the grief, but I sure as hell wouldn't feel good about it and knew it was something I'd have to live with forever.

The old man came out with his kettle of beans and salt pork and set it on the ground and then went back in and came out with three tin plates and some spoons and another jug of whiskey.

"Dig in," he said. "Ain't nothing formal round here."

So we ate till our bellies felt like they were full of buckshot, except the Cap'n didn't eat but a spoonful or two.

"Ain't it to your liking?" the old man asked.

"It is, I'm just not feeling up to snuff is all," the Cap'n replied.

To be honest, I wanted to say it was about the worst meal I ever ate, but I held my tongue in order to be polite.

Afterward we smoked and the old man said, "What you all going to Finger Bone for?"

It wasn't common for one man to ask another his business, but there wasn't anything overly common about this old buzzard. I just supposed he was lonely for talk.

The Cap'n said, "Buy some horses."

"Horses, huh?"

The Cap'n nodded as if to say, *What part of that don't you understand, old-timer?*

The old man pushed the jug toward the Cap'n and he tipped it up, and I could see the liquor was beginning to take its effect on him from eating so little and drinking that hard whiskey.

"We best turn in," I suggested. It was nigh on full dark now, stars beginning to sprinkle the sky and a half moon rising over the rimrock.

"Go on, make yourselves to home," the old man said, standing away and stretching. Then he hooked a forefinger through the jug's ear and took it up and swallowed what little was yet still in it and said, "You boys sleep well." Then he trudged off inside his door and closed it.

"I'm about all in, Jim," Cap'n said.

"Let's go saw some wood then," I replied, and we stood up and walked to the shed and pitched down some saddle blankets hanging from a nail hook onto the thicket of straw there.

"Boy, it feels like I've swallowed a belly full of bent nails," Cap'n said as he lay down. "It's pretty bad how life treats you when you get old . . ."

In a few minutes I could hear him breathing like a man will when he's first asleep. I was myself tired but not so much, and I lay there in the darkness with only a little of the moon's light coming in over the partial shed wall above my head.

I kept thinking about Luz, and how it would feel to be lying with her tonight in a regular bed and when was I ever going to get too old or tired of sleeping on the ground or some old man's shed floor and finally settle down permanent? I vowed once I got back home again, that was it for me; it would take hell and high water to ever get me to do anything like this again. Jesus himself could ride up to my place and say he needed help with the Philistines and I wouldn't go with him.

I was thinking all this when I must have drifted off to sleep, for I suddenly started awake when I heard the crunch of boot just outside the shed.

Chapter Eight

THE BOYS

Billy said after the funeral of their stepdad, Jardine Frost, when he and Sam went off behind the saloon in town after asking the drunk, Thompson, to buy them a bottle and giving him a dollar to do it: "We ought to skin out of this town."

Sam, barely fourteen, was still weighing the loss of the only daddy he knew with an ounce of kindness in him. Jardine never beat them, never laid into them, real soft-spoken sort and good to their ma as well. Would come riding home some days after his job as a horse trader with bouquets of wildflowers he'd stop and pick and sometimes bags of rock candy for the boys. One time he came home with a baseball for them. It was a treat to wait for Jardine to come home from his work.

But then one day he didn't come home till some men brought him home in the back of a wagon wrapped in a tarp, saying how he'd gotten into an argument with a fellow over a horse the fellow claimed Jardine sold him that had the bloat and how Jardine refused to refund the fellow's money and how the fellow went up the street and got drunk and came back with a long barrel pistol and shot Jardine through his rib meat, the first round, and the second through the back of his "goddamn skull" to quote the fellow who shot him. The fellow was arrested and a quick trial was held and the fellow was found innocent of murder in the first degree and every other degree because nobody could prove one way or the other whether it was a justified shooting or not, seeing as how the horse in question actually had the bloat and in fact died only one hour before Jardine was himself shot.

So there he now lay in a cold dark grave with nothing but Billy and Sam's memory of him photographed in their minds, this mild-mannered fellow with eyes blue as ice water, closed forever against the stain of the world wherein men could shoot you over practically nothing at all and get away with it.

"Where would we go?" Sam asked when Billy suggested they leave Tascosa. "And what about Ma?"

"Ma can make out a lot easier she don't have our hungry mouths to feed. We'd be doing her a favor."

"How'd we make a living and feed our own hungry mouths?" Sam asked.

"Hell if I know, but we'll make out one way or the other."

Billy was nineteen, and growing up as he had, with a mother who couldn't pick the right man till she picked Jardine, or rather, Jardine picked her, had made him grow up fast.

He passed the whiskey bottle to Sam, and Sam took a hit off it while Billy rolled them a shuck and smoked it first, then handed it to Sam when Sam handed him back the bottle.

"You know that son of a bitch Longly that killed Jardine and got away with it ought to pay something for his sin," Billy said.

"How you mean?"

"I mean he ought to pay something."

"Like what?"

"I don't know, but we ought to ride over there and make him pay something to Ma, and to us."

"How we gone do that? We ain't even got no horse to ride over there with."

"We got the keys to the padlock that holds the gate to those horses Jardine was trading for that man in Uvalde."

"You mean steal us some?"

"You think that fellow from Uvalde when he gets here is just gone give us two horses for showing up and asking him?"

"No, I don't reckon he would."

"We got Jardine's pistols," Billy said. "We'll need 'em."

Sam remembered the Remingtons Jardine kept in a red velvet-lined case made of mahogany he'd shown them once from his old days of being a town marshal in Dallas. The citizens there had given him the set for his faithful duty of keeping law and order. They were even inscribed on the backstraps with *J. R. Frost.*

"His prize pistols?" Sam said.

"You think he's gone need them anymore?"

"No, I reckon not."

"Time we went out on our own, became men," Billy said. "Pass me that shuck."

They drank half the whiskey before Sam puked up his portion and slumped down green. Billy, nearly fallen-down drunk, laughed at his little half brother.

That night after they'd all gone to bed, Billy woke Sam and told him to pack some things and off they snuck out the back door with Jardine's prize pistols stuck inside their belts and walked clear to town where Jardine kept the man from Uvalde's horses locked up in a corral with a big brass padlock.

Billy undid the lock with Jardine's key, and they

slipped inside among the horses, some of whom slept standing, their heads down. Billy picked his way through the small herd to where some saddles and bridles were kept next to a big grain bin.

"Pick you out one," Billy whispered.

They each took a bridle and saddle and picked them out a horse and slipped the headstall over their horses' heads and the bit between their teeth and saddled them up, then walked them out slow through the gate, with Billy dismounting and locking the gate again before remounting, telling Sam to take it slow, to walk up the back alley behind the town's buildings till they hit the road leading south.

It was half a moon that night, enough to see by but not easily be seen unless somebody was looking for them.

When they reached the south road Billy said, "Okay, let's ride these sons a bitches like they was horses we just stole."

"We *did* just steal them," Sam said.

"My goddamn point exactly," Billy said with a grin.

They found Longly's place easy enough. Just a lone little shack looked like a shadow in the half light of night, sitting just off the road three miles outside of town.

"What if he keeps a dog?" Sam said. "And it sets to barking loud."

"Then I feel sorry for that old dog," Billy said

and pulled the Remington out of his waistband, and holding it like that, knowing what he might end up doing with it, gave him a whole other feeling than he'd ever had before.

"You best pull your piece too."

Sam followed suit and they rode up to the house slow, thinking any minute some hound would come out barking and snarling. And such would have been the case, but Longly's hound had been bitten a week earlier by a rattlesnake several times and died an anguished death. The man Longly had not yet replaced him, much to Billy and Sam's good fortune and not to Longly's.

They tied off their mounts out front, and Billy stepped up to the door with Sam across from him, both of them holding their pistols at the ready. Billy rapped hard at the door and kept rapping till a light came on inside.

"Who is it?" they could hear a man calling from within. "Who the hell is there and what do you want?"

Billy shouted, "It's the law, open this goddamn door!"

It opened slowly and Billy stuck the muzzle of his revolver in Longly's face and walked him back into the room with Sam following.

"You're the brats of that whore Frost was living with," he said, and Billy struck him across the ear with the barrel of Jardine's pistol, and Longly yelped like someone had scalded him.

Sam was feeling nervous.

"Give me all your money, you son of a bitch," Billy commanded. "What you owe my family for taking the life of a decent man."

Longly held his bleeding ear, the blood dripping through his fingers and down his hand to his wrist.

"I'll give you shit and call it money, is what I'll do, you mealymouth little peckerwood."

Billy struck him again, across the collarbone, and dropped the man to his knees. Billy thumbed back the hammer and put the muzzle to the man's head and said, "You think I won't, just go ahead and call me another name and find out."

Longly relented, and Billy let him get a tin box from under his bed and take out the money he had in it, then Billy ordered Sam to take a rope and tie Longly to the bed, and Sam did what Billy told him. And once he had Longly tied to the bed, Billy went into the small kitchen and broke off a table leg and come back in and set to whaling on the bound man till Longly stopped screaming, passed out from the blows.

"I reckon playing all that baseball come in handy, huh?" Billy said, standing there breathless.

"You killed him," Sam muttered.

"Nah, I didn't. I just busted him up good. Look, he's still breathing fine. Let's get."

So they left with Longly's money and the man from Uvalde's horses and Jardine's pistols and Longly's canned peaches and a slab of fatback bacon and coffee in a burlap poke tied to Sam's saddle horn, and Billy wanted to burn the place to the ground with Longly still in it, but Sam talked him out of it.

And they rode hard for a time but then Billy said, "We ain't safe nowhere this side of the border, we best go to Old Mexico, cross the river and get on down to where they don't care who we are or what we've done."

And along the way they sustained themselves by holding up small stores to get supplies, and once a saloon for whiskey and a box of cigars. They even robbed a bank in Brazos but hardly got more than pocket change because all the money was kept in a large steel vault the banker said couldn't be opened till the next morning.

They camped out in canyons so nobody looking could see their firelight. They drank the whiskey till they passed out from it and smoked the cigars till they got used to smoking them.

One night while thus camped, Sam said, "I miss Ma."

"I miss her too," Billy said. "And as soon as we get a little extra money, we'll send her some of it to help her along and let her know we're all right."

Sam sometimes wept in his sleep.

And once they got down near the border, Billy said, "Time you and me became full-fledged desperadoes."

"How do you mean?" Sam said. "I thought we already were with all the crimes we been committing."

"We stole things, yeah—whiskey, horses, and even a box of cigars, and robbed that bank in Brazos." They both laughed at the fiasco of it. Billy continued, "And we come close to killing a man—which is the truest mark of a true desperado," Billy said. "But we ain't blooded yet."

"How do we get blooded?"

They were sitting their horses atop a rocky ridge looking down on a small village below. And perhaps a mile or two beyond, if their judgment was worth a spit, lay the river that once you crossed you were in Old Mexico. The river shone like a wire in the fading light.

"Come on, I'll show you," Billy said and spurred his mount down the slope, and Sam followed him on down.

They rode into the village with their pistols plainly showing, and folks outside their haciendas stopped to look at them. It was just one dusty street leading up to small adobes on either side, ramadas with roofs made of ocotillo that threw down patches of striped shade. They came to a cantina halfway up the street, and Billy said, "Let's rein in here."

They tied off their horses and went in without trying to hide the fact they were wearing pistols, and strode to the plank bar. A small, thin man with a horseshoe of gray hair stood behind the bar.

"We'd like some whiskey and a woman."

The man looked from Billy to Sam.

"You boys got a red cent to pay for the booze and pussy?"

The man had a deep Southern drawl.

"I guess we wouldn't be standing here asking for it if we couldn't pay for it," Billy said, and slapped five silver dollars on the table. "What'll that get us?"

The man smiled enough to show he had buck teeth.

"Zee!" he called to a woman seated at a table by herself on the other side of the room. Near where she sat, a man sat with his head lying down on his table, snoring.

She was a lot bigger than anyone else in the room, and she lifted that bulk from her chair and came over. She was wearing a loose, thin cotton shift that showed the outline of her breasts and the patch of dark hair between her legs when she waddled over.

"These boys say they want a piece of beaver," and he pointed at the money on the bar. "What do you think, Zee?"

She looked at each of them.

"You little peckers think you're up to handling Mama Zee?" she said.

"I reckon we're about up for anything," Billy said.

"Shit then, follow me."

"I'll wait here," Sam said.

"Hell you will," Billy said and tugged him by his collar to follow the woman out back to a small shack that was barely large enough for a bed and a basin, which was all there was in it.

"How you peckers want it, one at a time or both together?" he said.

"One at a time," Billy said.

"Strip off your duds then, or if you'd rather, leave 'em on, but let's get started because it's tight in here and I don't mean this," she said, lifting the shift above her fat thighs. "I'm not laying in this stifling room any longer than necessary."

Sam cut his gaze away as Billy dropped his pants and climbed on top of the woman. Sam wished he could shut his ears as well—the ache of bedsprings and the woman grunting like a shoat hog. Then Billy climbed off and said, "Your turn."

It was something awful and at the same time fixating, Sam thought as he tried not to think at all. And when it was finished he and Billy went back into the bar while the woman cleaned herself up standing over the washbasin and had themselves a shot of tequila each, then left and headed for the river.

And when they'd crossed the river and made camp for the night, Billy said, "How was that back there?"

"Plain ugly," Sam said.

"Yeah, but you liked it too, didn't you?"

"I guess it's second best to using your hand."

Billy laughed and said, "Well, we're both blooded now."

"I feel like I ought to jump in that river and warsh."

"Go ahead."

"Think I will."

"Hell, I'll join you."

And for a time, as the sun sank beyond the brown hills, they frolicked in the cool waters of the river like fishes until they were exhausted and climbed out and lay on the grass naked and wet, semi happy knowing they'd probably never cross north of the river again—that what had been home was home no more.

Billy lay on the grass thinking, *I guess what we have done can never be undone. I should have left Sam out of this, but too late, too late.*

The stars looked like God's own eyes staring down at him.

Sam said, "I hope we didn't catch the pox from that fat whore."

"What do you know about the pox?" Billy said.

"Nothing, except it's supposed to be something bad and something you get from whores. I heard it makes men go crazy and some blind. I heard old Wild Bill Hickok had it and he went near blind, and that's how come that fellow shot him in

Deadwood City because Bill couldn't even see the fellow pull his pistol."

"I don't think we caught the pox, do you?" Billy said.

"I don't know."

They closed their eyes and fell silent, each wrapped in his own thoughts. A coyote yipped from somewhere off in the dark hills. Another yipped back.

Chapter Nine

JIM & THE CAP'N

I eased my Merwin Hulbert from my holster and brought it out and ready waiting for the next footstep to crunch into the caliche. The Cap'n lay asleep, his snores light, rhythmic. I leaned and touched his shoulder, and he awoke instantly, sitting up, his hand full of pistol. I touched the back of his wrist to keep him from firing at me.

"Someone's outside," I whispered.

We didn't hear anything.

"Maybe nothing," I said.

Then we heard it again, something, someone moving around outside. I rolled away from the Cap'n so that I was pressed up against the wall of the shed nearest the sound. There was a slight crack between the weathered boards and I put my eye to it. The moon was bright enough to show a shadow of a man carrying an ax standing there several inches from the shed as though listening for us. I shifted back to the Cap'n and whispered, "Start snoring again," then rolled back to the wall as soon as he did.

As I watched through the crack, the figure outside simply stood there holding the ax down alongside his leg, and the hair on the back of my neck rose. But it rose even more when a second figure appeared and stood next to the first. He was also carrying something in his hands—a shotgun it looked like, judging by the short length of it. I heard them whispering.

"You know what to do," the one said to the other. It was the voice of the old man who a couple of hours earlier shared his grub and whiskey with us. I guess he was about to put an end to all that hospitality. They took a single step forward toward the shed and I shot the old man, the flash of light blinding my night vision for a moment.

I heard a yelp and the Cap'n crawled over quickly and said, "What's going on?"

But instead of answering him I kicked down the loose boards of the wall and fanned the hammer of my pistol into the body of the man with the ax who'd paused and bent to his fallen comrade. I was pretty sure I hit him four out of four because every shot coming in rapid fire as it did caused his body to jump and jerk. He dropped the ax with the second round, spun completely around with the third, and went down with the fourth. The old man was on the ground moaning. The Cap'n was right there, his gun held straight out in front of him, cocked and ready.

"Get a lantern if you would, Cap'n," I said. He crossed the yard to the house and took a bull's-eye that had been hanging next to the door on a nail and struck a match to the wick, then lowered the glass and brought it near the two shot men.

One, the one holding the ax, was a younger version of the old man. He was shot through the belly and writhing on the ground, groaning through clenched teeth.

"Bring your light over here to this other one," I said, and the Cap'n walked it over and lowered it to the old man's face. His eyes were crossed in death as though he'd been trying to look down his nose at where my bullet struck him—top button of his shirt. Cap'n flashed the light around the ground till it fell on the double barrel. He bent and picked it up and looked at it close. Then he looked at the one moaning and groaning and said, "You chickenshit son of a bitch. How many others you done this way?"

He gasped and said, "I need a doctor, oh . . . oh . . ."

"You're gut shot, among your other wounds,"

I said. "A doctor won't do you any good."

It was a mean goddamn thing to say to someone dying, but I owed him no sympathy for trying to waylay me and the Cap'n.

"Oh . . . help me . . ."

"You bought the ticket, now do the dance," I said and stood away.

Cap'n, still carrying the shotgun in his hand, his pistol now tucked down in his holster, said, "The old man must have thought we had money we were going to use to buy horses," he said. "I wonder who this other'n is."

"Looks enough like the old man I'd say he was kin, son or something."

"I don't guess it really matters, does it?"

"No sir, I don't suppose at this point it really does."

"What do you want to do about him?" Cap'n said, pointing the barrels of the shotgun at the dying man, whose boot heels kept digging for purchase into the ground.

"Leave him," I said. "He'll not make it till daylight."

"Can't just leave him like that, Jim. Wouldn't hardly be Christian."

I looked at the Cap'n as he handed me the shotgun.

"No, I'm not going to kill him," I said.

"I know," the Cap'n said. "I know you ain't, Jim." Then the Cap'n stood over the wounded man and drew his pistol quickly and shot him through the skull, and reholstered his revolver.

"I didn't see no other way, did you?" the Cap'n said.

"None at all."

"What time you figure it is?"

"Two, three in the morning," I reckon.

"Still can catch a few hours of rest and head out first light," he said.

"All right, if you think you can after all this."

"Might just as well make use of that bed inside," he said. "Beats hell out of sleeping in the shed like a couple of dogs."

"Be my guest. I'll wait out here 'case there's any more of his boys comes home."

"There won't be," Cap'n said. "I think we done all the killing tonight we're meant to."

The Cap'n went inside and I took out my makings and rolled myself a shuck to ease off the things I was feeling. Then I took the dead men by their boots and dragged them both into the shed and laid them there, and went out again and sat down on one of the supper chairs that was still out front.

I never have found out all the reasons that possess men to set upon one another, money, hatred, just pure meanness. Whatever it is gets in a fellow's mind makes no sense if in the end the man you set upon puts a bullet through your brain.

I smoked my shuck down, and then I guess I

dozed fitfully in the chair until first dawn. The sky was as gray as a ghost with just a seam of silver light between it and the horizon. I went inside to wake the Cap'n, but he was already awake, but just lying there. He sat up and said, "Was it a dream I had about last night, me shooting a fellow in the brains?"

"No sir, it was real enough," I said.

He rubbed his eyes, then pulled on his boots, and we went outside again. We went out to the pump and washed our hands and faces and strung water through our hair, and then went back inside, where I fixed us some breakfast of fatback and beans from a can. We ate there at the table without speaking anymore about last night till we finished and stood away from the table and went outside again, leaving the dishes just setting there.

I saddled my horse and then put the Cap'n's in the traces of the hack, and he climbed aboard and looked off toward the road and said, "What'd you do with the bodies, Jim?"

"I put them in the shed."

He nodded.

"The wolves and coyotes smell death, they'll be round soon enough."

"I'm not that far gone as a human being yet to let them have at dead men," I said. I went over to the shed and searched around till I found a can of coal oil, then shook out the contents all over the boards before striking a match and setting the whole place afire, the bodies still inside. The fire caught slowly at first, then built quickly enough, like a maw of flame swallowing everything.

We rode off toward Finger Bone, the hungry flames behind us just as if we were riding out of Sodom and Gomorrah.

"I wonder how many others them two has waylaid over the years?" the Cap'n said as we rode along.

I said I didn't know but I guessed we weren't the first, that they just didn't suddenly start with us, because of the way the old man had set it up.

"I'm surprised he didn't try and drug us with that whiskey first," Cap'n said.

"You and me both know, criminals was smart, wouldn't none of them get jailed or shot," I said.

"Well, their souls are with Jesus now," he said.

"I doubt Jesus will have any truck with them," I said.

"I doubt it too, Jim. I doubt it too."

We were leaving death to go and create more of it, and that was an unsettling thought if ever there was one.

It was like death was dogging us just so it could learn how to do it proper. Last night, when I shot that man, I realized then and there, I didn't flinch at the thought, my heart never quickened, my hand never wavered, and it made me realize that in whatever ways I thought I'd changed, I hadn't changed all that much.

The road lay long and straight ahead of us, the sun just now rising above the rimrock to our rear, and the world seemed no wiser or bereft because of what we'd left in our wake.

Chapter Ten

BILLY & SAM

They wandered from place to place, striking up friendships with the locals because they were in a strange country and Billy had heard some tales from Jardine back when Jardine was still alive and talking about the things that went on in Old Mexico. Said he'd been there a time or two, back in his wild youth, Jardine called it. "It's easy country if you know how to get along with the natives," he'd said. "Hard country if you don't.

"Me and some of my pals went down there that first time to see could we steal some Mexican mustangs off a big ranch down there. Ah, hell, we were only half-baked boys without no mothers and fathers. Most of us jumped off the orphan trains rather than be put to work as slaves for some farmer or rancher. We had to grow up hard and do what we could to survive. But it ain't no sort of way to live, boys. That's why I want to be a pa to you—to show you there is a better way. And I love hell out of your ma, too."

Jardine always had good stories to tell, and Billy and Sam would listen raptly as Jardine told them. He always wore a workshirt buttoned to the top button winter and summer and was fastidious about having clean hands, would wash them ten, twelve times a day and clean under his fingernails.

"So we get on down there," Jardine said of that particular time, "and first thing we did was come into this little town where all the women were as pretty as young colts and batting their eyes at us, me and Clarence Harper and Gil Westmore, and not a one of us over the age of seventeen, eighteen years old, and still green peckerwoods as you'd ever find.

"We practically fell out of our saddles from looking at them and having them look at us. Then some big-bellied man standing out front of a cantina waved us over and we stopped to see what he wanted and the son of a gun, and I swear this is the God's honest truth, had nothing but gold teeth in his mouth." Billy remembered how Jardine would shake his head over something he found hard to believe even when he was the one saying it was true. Jardine showed them his own teeth for emphasis.

"This fellow owned the cantina and a cathouse as it proved out. You boys know what a cathouse is?"

Billy and Sam shook their heads, and Jardine grinned and looked round to make sure their ma wasn't anywhere within earshot.

"It's a place where a man can buy himself a whore," Jardine said and waited for the effect to take hold of them, and when they both grinned he continued, "Anyways he says to us, 'Hey, gringos, you want some tequila. Real cheap, ten cents a glass, and I got some nice women, real cheap too.' And he called some of them outside there on the veranda of his cantina and we liked to have fallen over because she wasn't nowhere near the beauty of the ones we'd been seeing till then. She was real skinny for one thing, and not very good-looking unless you squinted. She was wearing nothing but these little cotton shifts you could see the dark of her tits through. Had this straight chopped-off hair and stuttered when she talked."

Billy and Sam tried hard to see it in their minds: the ugly woman standing on the Mexican's veranda in a cotton gown so thin her dark tits showed through.

"Well, I won't go into any of the dirty details," Jardine said. "Let's just say me and Clarence and Gil had us one heck of a time for a couple of days there even if we had to stay drunk as sailors. We went in that place with about forty dollars in money in our pockets and come out picked clean as chickens, with hangovers the size of Montana. We ended up crossing back north of the river with nary a stolen horse or a centavo to our names. But we was burning up with desire to go back again soon as we could put a little stake together. But then Clarence got hitched to a gal he got in the family way, and Gil got drowned in the Canadian River trying to cross where the ice was thin that winter. He was trying to save a yearling that had fallen in."

"What about the other time you went to Old Mexico?" Billy asked that time.

Jardine simply shook his head and said, "Boys, you don't even want to know about that time. Let's just leave it at it wasn't nothing like the first time. And you'll learn soon enough, nothing ever is." Then he showed them a puckered scar just below his shoulder. "That's all that needs to be said about the second time I went into Old Mexico." They knew it was a bullet wound that had left the scar.

"Remember some of those stories Jardine told us about?" Billy said as they rode along a white dust road with the sun straight over their heads.

Sam smiled and said, "I sure do. Wouldn't it be something if we could find that Mexican with the gold teeth that ran that cathouse and give that same skinny gal a go like he did?"

"It sure enough would," Billy said. "We'd have to get drunk like he did, but we'd get her done, wouldn't we!"

They both laughed. But neither could remember

where or if Jardine had said the name of the town, and all they could do was hope that each town they came to might be *that* town. Some of the smaller villages didn't even have a cantina.

Soon enough they ran low on their luck, their pockets nearly empty and sitting in the shade of a ramada, sharing some tamales they'd bought from a local woman.

Sam said, "What's our next play?"

Billy shrugged. A grungy hound had come sniffing around, its coat dirty and rough. Billy broke off a piece of the tamale and fed it to the dog.

"Now git," Billy said and the dog slunk off.

"I guess we need to rob something," Billy said.

Sam looked around at the small, dusty village.

"Rob what?" Sam said. "There ain't nothing here."

"Not here, but maybe the next place we come to. A store or a bank. Might even rob a railroad train if we come up on one going slow enough."

"Railroad train," said Sam incredulously.

"Well, something. I don't know what yet till we get to it."

Their boots were dusty with the white dust and so were their jeans.

"It's pleasant country, ain't it?" Billy said.

"I reckon. You miss Ma?"

"Some," Billy said.

"I do."

96

Billy ate the last of his tamale and wiped his hands on his jeans. "Eat up," he said. "We still got some daylight to burn."

"How you think Jardine got shot that time he was down here?" Sam said, still chewing his tamale.

"Hell if I know. Probably did something with a married woman and her husband shot him over it." Billy grinned at the thought. "Knowing Jardine, how wild he said he used to be in his youth, it wouldn't surprise me now, would it you?"

Sam shook his head. "I miss him too," Sam said, swallowing the last little piece of his meal.

"Yeah, well, we pretty well took care of that son of a bitch who killed him, didn't we?"

Sam didn't say anything but instead stood up from the shade and went over and tightened the cinch on his horse.

The sun burned through his shirt, drying the sweat stains, and he told himself as he fixed the saddle that he sure didn't feel fourteen anymore, but felt more like a grown man, him and Billy running all over the country taking what they needed and living free like they were, probably wanted outlaws north of the river so's they could never go back. It left a bad taste in his mouth thinking about it, and in some ways he regretted ever having taken off with Billy in the first place.

Finally he put a foot in his stirrup, realizing he didn't have a say in things now, things had gone too far for either of them to have a say in it. They could quit and turn themselves in to the law back north of the river and get locked up in a jail, or they could just keep going and see what happened.

The other thing troubling him was it seemed to hurt when he pissed.

"I think I caught the pox from that fat whore," he said as they turned their horses out to the road again heading south. He mentioned how it hurt when he went.

"I'd say it's a sure sign," Billy said. "I think I got it too. Started out tickling a little and now it feels like I'm trying to piss razor blades. We'll look for a doctor the next town we come to."

"Can you die from it, the pox?"

Billy shrugged.

"I never heard of nobody dying from it. But I did hear it can drive a man insane, he carries it in his blood long enough."

"It's like our own sins are eating us up," Sam said.

Billy looked over at him.

"Shut up," he said.

"Hell," Sam said. "I don't guess I have to if I don't want to."

Chapter Eleven

The wind-waggled sign read: CIUDAD DE TONTOS. A sagebrush tumbled wildly across the road.

"What's it mean?" Sam asked.

"I look Mescan to you?" Billy said.

"Hell, I figured when you were running with that Mescan gal back home you knew some of the lingo."

"I knew enough to say let me kiss your lips and feel your titties," Billy said with a grin.

They spurred their mounts forward. It was a good-size town set between twin mountains whose slopes were prickled with hundreds of saguaro cactus.

Most of the buildings were adobe, low slung and whitewashed so it hurt the eyes to look at them under the blazing sun. Judging by where it stood, it was sometime late afternoon, four or five o'clock.

"You think maybe there's a doctor here we can get ourselves checked out and fixed up?" Sam said.

"I reckon, if we had something to pay him with."

"I'd trade my pistol for some relief."

"You'd be a damn fool then. In this country."

"I can't hardly stand to sit my saddle."

They reined in at a merchant store.

"What we aim to do here?" Sam said. "We got no money."

"We'll figure it out," Billy said and dismounted.

Sam followed suit and followed Billy inside. It was quiet and cool inside the store, with the scent of dry wood and blankets, coffee and tea.

Nobody was in sight.

"We could just grab some things and go," Sam said.

"That's what I was thinking. See can you find a gunny and then put some of them canned goods on that shelf yonder in it."

"What you gone do?"

Billy was eyeing a big brass cash register.

"What you think I'm gone do?"

Billy went around the other side of the counter, keeping an eye peeled for whoever owned the place while Sam poked around for a gunny till he came up with one.

"Eureka!" he said.

"Keep quiet," Billy said as he punched the buttons on the cash register in an effort to get the drawer to pop open. Finally it did with a ring and the drawer popped out. But the money was Mexican money, paper and copper and silver pesos.

"Shit," muttered Billy, but scooped them out and stuffed what was there in his pockets while Sam hustled cans of peaches and pears, beans and potted meats into the gunny.

Billy saw a rack of rifles across the way and went over but the rifles were chained to the rack and held with a padlock and he wondered where the key was.

"I can't believe this, can you?" Sam was saying when they heard something from behind a door that stood to the rear of the store. They froze listening.

"What was that?"

"I don't know but we best get in the wind," Billy said.

Then they heard something else, a sharp cry of pain sounded like a woman crying out.

"Something's wrong," Sam said.

"Don't worry about it, let's get the hell out of here."

"No, somebody's hurt back yonder."

"It's not our problem unless we make it our problem," Billy said, tugging at the gunny Sam was holding, trying to pull him toward the door.

"No, it wouldn't be right to let a woman lay back there hurt." Sam started for the door, then they heard the sound of breaking glass and a loud crash and Sam pulled the pistol from his belt and cocked it and Billy said, "You're a crazy son of a bitch you go through that door."

But Sam went through it anyway and Billy yanked his piece and followed his kid brother, figuring he couldn't just leave Sam hanging like that.

What they saw on the floor stopped them dead in their tracks: a woman lying in a pool of blood, gasping, her dress torn away, everything exposed, and several bloody stab wounds in her chest.

"Jesus God!" Sam said.

Billy saw the torn dress lying to the side and grabbed it and knelt by the woman, pressing the folded cloth to the woman's torso to try and stanch the flow of blood. She looked at him wild-eyed and gasped, only the gasp was more a rattling gurgle than anything.

Sam stood frozen, gun in his hand as Billy struggled to stop the blood. The woman squirmed and Sam shouted, "She's dying, Billy!"

"Goddamn, help me with this. Do something."

But neither of them knew what to do, and Billy looked into the frightened eyes of the woman that stared at him with so much fear, it went straight into him. His hands were soaked in blood up to his wrists now, the dress soaked too so that you could wring the blood out of it, and Billy thought, *How much blood can a body have?*

Sam ran out into the store and grabbed a striped blanket from a shelf and came back and pressed it to the woman's nakedness even as she thrashed about in her agony.

"Please, lady," Billy was saying. "Please . . ." Then he looked at Sam and said, "Run get somebody, see can you find a doctor, anybody."

But when Sam turned there stood a man in a tan soldier's uniform with a tan cap, clearly a uniform, and the man was nearly as tall as the doorjamb. He had dark fierce eyes and long black mustaches and wore a pistol in a black holster with a flap over it he'd already unbuttoned and was pulling the pistol from.

He spoke to them harshly in Spanish and aimed his pistol at them, waving them away from the body. Then he came and knelt next to the woman and spoke her name, "Maria . . ." They saw her eyes roll toward the man as if she was trying to speak to him with her eyes.

More Mexican soldiers poured into the room, their guns drawn.

"Shit," Billy said.

Then the woman shuddered and the man cried out to some of the other soldiers in Spanish and they came and lifted her and carried her out of the room in a hurry.

"You killed my child," the man said to Billy and Sam in English while the remaining soldiers kept their guns leveled at the boys.

"No sir!" Billy said. "We didn't have nothing to do with this."

"You little shits!"

The tall man stood, stepped forward, and slapped

Sam with an open hand hard enough across the face to stagger him. Then he cocked the pistol and put it against Billy's head.

"Maybe I blow out your brains, eh."

Billy closed his eyes expecting the bullet. But then the man finally growled something to the others, and before Billy or Sam knew what was happening, they were dragged from the store and up the street to a large adobe building with bars on some of the windows. Even then the streets had suddenly filled with people, the word having gone out that Señorita Toro, the General's youngest daughter, had been murdered, her throat slit, that she had been "*violado*," they whispered. The rumors were rampant. Of course they were wrong on some of the facts, but what were facts when such a thing happened?

The General had been at home eating a meal when his brother-in-law, his wife's brother, came rushing in breathlessly to tell him there had been trouble at the store.

"What sort of trouble?" the General said. He'd been eating a chicken.

"Very bad trouble," the brother-in-law said.

"Maria, is she all right?"

"I don't know," the brother-in-law said. "You know I just left for a little while to go get lunch and when I returned I saw two hombres there in the back room with her on the floor. They both had pistols, and, well . . . I came right away for you."

The General stood with such a burst of energy he knocked over the table and the platter of chicken and everything else and grabbed his cap, hurrying after his brother-in-law toward the store, telling him as they went to go and round up some of his men and have them hurry to the store.

What he saw broke his heart when he entered.

His lovely and beloved Maria, her bare legs sticking out from under a blanket, the pool of blood flowing outward across the wood planks of the floor. He bent and took the blanket away from her and saw the numerous stab wounds, the two boys with blood on their hands. He'd pulled his pistol and ordered them to stand away from her, then knelt next to his daughter.

"Oh, dios querido!"

Then he'd wanted to know why these gringos did this thing but they denied having anything to do with it, and he became instantly angry and slapped the one boy hard across the face and nearly shot them. But instead his logic took over and he ordered some of his men to take the girl to the infirmary and the others to place the boys in jail until he could learn the truth of what had happened.

He told himself that if his child died, he would immediately execute the two boys without benefit of a trial. He would have them shot by firing squad; he himself would take up a rifle and make sure they paid for their crime.

105

He was at once angry and aggrieved, and the two emotions struggled within him to find some balance.

For now, he must go to the infirmary and await the outcome.

At his advanced age, he had learned it is always best to keep your anger at bay until all the facts were known and then proceed with due speed to bring about justice where wrongs were committed.

But it was hard not to want to kill those two muchachos then and there.

Very damn hard.

Chapter Twelve

Of course the General had them beaten to get them to confess to their crime, to say why they did it. The men who did the beating tied Billy and Sam to chairs and hit repeatedly with a leather strap that cut and stung until their heads rang. At one point the General himself did it.

"What I want to know is, why did you come here and do this thing?" he said to them in between the beatings, between the buckets of water poured into their bloody mouths until they choked and almost drowned.

"We didn't!" Billy sputtered. "We found her like that."

"Oh, is this why you had her blood all over your hands, eh?"

The General's English was quite good. He was by far the most threatening of the many men who stood in the room along the walls looking on with passive faces.

Billy tried to explain it, so did Sam. Tried explaining it over and over again. But whenever they tried explaining it, the General or one of his men would hit them with the razor strap.

"Why don't you just kill us then, you believe we did it?" Billy screamed against the pain at one point.

The General shook his head, wiped the sweat from his forehead with the sleeve of his shirt, and drank from a bottle of tequila.

"If my *hija* dies, you can count on it, amigo."

The boys continued to deny their involvement with the savagery.

"You just happened to be there by accident, is that it? You came in and found her like that, is that your story?"

More beating.

Finally Billy said something that gave the General real pause: "If we done it, where's the damn knife we done it with!"

The General stayed the hand of his man holding the strap now.

"Did you find the knife?" he asked his men.

They looked at one another, shrugged, until an older man said, "No, General, but then we did not look or even think about it."

"Go and see if you can find the knife," the General ordered.

Several of them raced from the room and went to the store.

The strap stung like a razor being slashed across their skin. Sam couldn't help but cry. Billy bit the insides of his cheeks till they bled.

Then their mouths would be forced open and buckets of water would be poured down their throats until they thought they were drowning and would pass out, only to be awakened again, to be beaten again until they both thought they would go crazy.

"I did it!" Billy finally muttered. "I stabbed her for the money, but Sam didn't have nothing to do with it . . ." Billy couldn't take seeing Sam done that way; he knew if it kept up, Sam would probably die first. Sam didn't deserve any of what was happening to him, Billy told himself, and if he had to confess to try and save Sam's life, then that's what he would do. And did.

The General nodded his head slowly, looked round at his men with a sagging satisfaction that he had gotten the confession.

"Why did you do it?" the General asked. "Did you do it for the money or because she was just there and an easy target for you? I want to know why."

"Yes . . . ," Billy said, his will completely broken. What difference would it make what he confessed to? The General was bound to kill him either way.

"What is your name and where do you come from?" the General said. "I want to put it on your death certificate and send it to your mother. I want her to feel what I am feeling."

Billy told him the only true name he knew of, his mother's maiden name, because he didn't really know who his father was or even who Sam's father was—both men had fled before they were born. And it wasn't right in his book to use Jardine's name, because Jardine was no kin at all; he was just a dead man lying in a grave with all those stories left untold.

"Billy Rogers," he said.

"And where do you come from Billy Rogers?"

"Tascosa, Texas."

"Tejas, eh?"

Billy nodded.

"Tell me your *madre*'s name and I will write and send her your death certificate and tell her how you have died from your sins here in Mexico. I'm a fair man."

"Don't have no living kin," Billy said. He could only imagine how hard his mother would take hearing that he and Sam had gotten themselves killed down in Mexico, accused of rape and murder. He didn't want her to have to bear that.

"So you come from the North and yet you have no family. Were you born of chickens? Hatched from eggs?"

The General motioned toward one of his men and said, "Kill that one," pointing at Sam. The soldier took out a black revolver and stepped forward.

"All right, damn it!" Billy said. "Her name's Laura Lee Rogers. And I'll tell you something else, you goddamn son of a bitch, you kill either of us, she send her daddy down here to wipe all you bastards out."

The General snorted his derision.

"This is what you think, that some old man will come down here for the sake of you two and himself be killed in the trying?"

"Gus Rogers is one mean son of a bitch," Billy declared. "And he'll bring every Ranger he knows down here and burn this town and hang you and all these others . . ."

Again, the General took pause. He knew a Gus Rogers from his youth who later joined the Texas Rangers and became well known on both sides of the border.

"So your *abuelo* is Gus Rogers, eh? You think he will come and save you two little shits? No, he won't save you. And if he tries I will have him buried in the same grave as you."

The General motioned for the Ruale to lower his weapon. Tears streamed down Sam's cheeks. It was so awful, the beating they'd given him, he'd just as soon be shot and put out of his misery.

"Put them in separate cells," the General ordered. Then he went out, and some of his men shadowed him because he was *the* General. He went first to the store where his men were searching for the knife.

"Have you found anything?"

"No, General."

"Keep looking."

"Yes, General."

"And wash that stain."

"Yes, General."

The General was full of sorrow for his young daughter, the issue of his third wife as it turned out. He'd been married before, and one wife had died in childbirth and the baby as well, and the other had gone off with a young vaquero and disappeared after giving birth to a daughter, Edwina, and left him to raise her alone, and she was nearly grown by the time he met his third wife, a young woman forty years his junior named Phillipina with whom he'd had, very late in his life, this child that now lay in the infirmary possibly dying.

He went home to tell his wife what had happened and she wept bitterly.

He said simply, "I'm sorry. I've caught those

who've done this thing and will see that they are punished severely." It seemed to the General too little consolation.

It was this wife's brother, the one who had informed him of the tragic events, who owned the store originally. Maria had gone to work there at first to learn to become a business woman. She proved very good at it due to her education at a girls' academy while an adolescent. It was at the General's wife's insistence that he bought the store outright from the brother-in-law, who'd gotten himself into gambling debt. The General gave the girl the deed and said, "It is yours," but again at his wife's insistence, the General let the brother-in-law stay on as an assistant to his daughter. And so it had been until this very day.

What of course the General could not have known was the effect that the lovely Maria would have on her uncle. How, having worked so closely with her day in and day out, Don Domingo had secretly observed the young woman's beauty, practically breathed it in and became intoxicated by it. How his passion for her was like a small flame that built into a raging fire. And how on that particular day the two young gringos had come into the store, he had already lured her into the storeroom and set upon her. And when she refused his advances, he put his knife to her breast and cut away the dress and threatened that she would give herself to him one way or the other, so impassioned was he. And that as he was finishing with her and they heard someone enter the front of the store, the ringing of the small bell above the door, this man, this Don Domingo, panicked when she cried out and plunged his knife into her several times. And then crashed through the tall window and ran down the alley.

No, the General would have never thought such a thing of his brother-in-law, the affable Don Domingo, who was by nature a quiet and unassuming man.

Absorbed as he was in his misery, the General waited with his wife at the infirmary; waiting, waiting, until she drew her final breath. Then the women who themselves were widows and prayed every day in the church came and said they would care for her. His wife, distraught beyond consolation, threw herself over the girl's body screaming, "No! No! No!"

The General could stand it no longer and wandered out into the night, then into the cantina, and proceeded to drink tequila while some of the men who always accompanied him stood by and watched somberly.

"What will you do, General?"

But he only wanted to erase the memory of seeing his daughter as he had—naked and terribly wounded and now peacefully dead. How does one wash away such a memory?

He fought the impulse to go straight to the jail

and kill them both. That would be too easy; they deserved greater punishment before he killed them. For what would they suffer in comparison to what Maria had suffered if he gave them each a quick bullet to the head? No, let them think about it, the hour of their death, in a way that his child had no time to think of her hour of death. Let them think about it and wonder when that hour would come to them. His military training had taught him much about how to punish the enemy. He would wait until after Maria's funeral.

He drank for a time, then said, "I want to go see the fortune-teller." His head was abuzz as though full of bees, from the absinthe and the tequila.

And so his soldiers walked him up the street to the house where the fortune-teller lived. The windows were dark. He rapped hard until a light came on and the door opened and the woman recognized her visitor.

"Sí, General," she said, and he removed his cap and heeled back the hair that had been sweated to his forehead and told her why he'd come. She invited him in, and he told his men to return and be with his grieving wife.

He stepped into the little house, and she led him to a settee and then sat in a chair near him and said, "Give me your hands, General." He extended them to her, and she turned them over and looked at his palms.

After a moment or two she released his hands.

"What do you think?" he said.

The fortune-teller said with all authority, "You have suffered greatly, but you will suffer even more . . ."

"Tell me how I could possibly suffer more than I am at this moment?"

She shook her head and said, "I don't know. It is not clear to me. But the lines in your palms tell of more trouble."

He gave a sigh and paid her for the fortune, stood and said, "Pack your things and be gone from this place by the morning."

His anger and pain were redoubled by the old woman's predictions. What did she know anyway? Everything around him seemed unpleasant; his life was ending in ruin.

And in those very hours while he was away from the jail, sitting at the infirmary and later in the saloon drinking, followed by his visit to the fortune-teller, the General could not have known that the old guard watching over the gringos was smitten with Billy. The old guard was of a secret nature, and his desire ran counter to most men. And when he first saw Billy, he began to speak to him in soft tones while Sam slept on the floor in the adjoining cell with his hands clamped between his knees.

This old guard said to Billy, "You are a very handsome boy." Billy had removed his shirt to inspect his welts and bruises. "Yes, very handsome. Would you like a cigarette?" At first Billy did not know what to make of this odd fellow who was old enough to be his grandfather, a man with small rat's eyes narrowly set into his thin face and greasy gray hair that lay plastered to his bulbous head when he removed his cap and combed it to one side with his dirty fingers. He had a sour smell to him.

But young Billy had good instincts for sin and so saw it as an opportunity even if he had to swallow down the bile created by his disgust of the old bastard's intentions.

And when the leering guard stood and went out into the outer office for something, Billy whispered to Sam, "I think I got a plan to get us out of here. You just be ready to go when it happens."

Sam started to ask a question but Billy silenced him with a finger to the lips.

"Just be ready to run when I make my play."

Sam nodded.

Then Billy kicked at the barred door till the old guard returned, his eyes bulging from his thick face.

Billy met his gaze as they stood separated by the bars.

"I need to use the privy," Billy said.

"I get you a bucket, amigo."

"No. I thought maybe we could go out back. You got a privy out back, don't you?" Then Billy glanced at Sam, who pretended to still be asleep.

"I don't want my brother to have to see anything," Billy whispered.

The guard nodded.

"Sí," he said. "We go out back, me and you."

The guard went and got a pair of manacles and put them through the bars and told Billy he must wear them.

Then he winked and said, "It's okay, you won't need your hands, hombre."

Sam watched through half-closed eyes the two of them going out the back door.

Chapter Thirteen

He waited till the old man had placed himself in a vulnerable position, then brought his manacled hands down hard, using the heavy cuffs to knock the guard senseless. The old man let out a hard groan after the first blow but did not make a sound when Billy struck him a second time, splitting open his head.

"You dirty son of a bitch!" Billy muttered, then took from around the man's neck the key that he'd used to unlock Billy's cell and rushed back inside. But the key would not fit or would not work the lock on Sam's cell. It was either the wrong key or the lock was jammed.

117

"Hurry up," Sam pleaded.

"I'm trying, goddamn it."

Sam was so frightened, his hands shook and his body trembled as Billy fumbled with the lock.

"It don't want to work," Billy said. "Goddamn it."

"Maybe there's another key somewhere."

Billy ran out into the jailer's room and searched through the drawers of the desk but could find no other keys. There was a shotgun sitting in the corner of the room and this he grabbed up, broke it open, saw that it was unloaded but held on to it anyway. He ran back into the cell area and tried the same key again, only in forcing it to try and open the lock he broke it off.

"Son of a bitch!" he yelped.

Sam looked at him through the bars with the saddest eyes Billy had ever seen on anyone.

They could hear approaching voices through a small open window there in the back.

"I'll have to come back for you," Billy said.

"No use to it," Sam said. "They'll kill me sure."

"No they won't. I won't let them." Billy touched Sam's hands that gripped the bars of his cage. "I'll come back."

Billy burned with guilt at having to leave Sam. He wanted to stay and fight but he had nothing to fight with. Two Ruales entered the jail through the front door. Both had been drinking heavily, and Billy could hear them talking loudly to each other. Billy fled out the back door, stepping over the prone body of the old guard, and ran down the darkened alley into the night.

Stealing a horse should be easy enough, he told himself as he ran away and came out at the far end, where he rounded a corner and stood in the shadows of the main street again. He could not tarry, he told himself. The Ruales would discover soon enough he'd escaped and sound the alarm. There were several saddle horses tied up on the street in front of a cantina. Billy was already formulating a plan in his head. The river was a good fifty miles north, but if he chose a good sound horse and rode like hell, he could make the river by daybreak, cross it, find the nearest town, and send a wire to his granddaddy.

He chose a big roan mare and knocked his heels into its flanks and rode it fast out of town and all night northward, resting only long enough for the horse to catch a blow and drink a little and eat a little. He'd read dime novels about the Pony Express riders and thought if they could ride at such a pace, so could he. He didn't care if he rode the horse to death as long as he could reach the river and cross over.

By dawn the next day that's exactly what he did, splashed across the river and into the States. He passed the dugout that had a sign crudely hand-painted that read: WHISKEY & ICE BEER and kept on riding. He needed to find a town that had a telegraph and remembered a town not many miles yet north of the river. And less than five miles more he came to a town with the funny name: Finger Bone. He learned from asking strangers where the telegraph was. He used his last dollar, that he'd stuck down inside his right boot for safekeeping, to send a telegram to his mother. Its contents explained in brief that Sam was in a Mexican jail in a place called Ciudad de Tontos —and that she should wire her daddy, Cap'n Rogers, and have him come quick with a company of Texas Rangers.

The last line of the telegram stated: *"I took blame to save Sam."* The telegrapher looked at him when he read it and said, "This true?"

"Just send it," Billy said.

Exhausted, he found a place to lie down in an alley to try and sleep and woke with a mangy dog licking his face. A dog with worse than dog's breath, and he sat up swatting at the creature. It yelped and growled once, then trotted off looking back over its shoulder at him.

"Boy, I'm piss poor and run down at the heels," he muttered to himself. The light in the alley-way was dim, indicating the sun was close to setting, he figured. He had no watch to tell time by. His welts and bruises felt like fishhooks in his flesh every time he moved. He stood with great effort. He'd been wise enough to have tied the reins of the stolen horse around his wrist before lying down. The horse stood with its head drooping, and he knew he'd pretty well worn it out on the hard ride.

He took pity on it knowing it wouldn't carry him another five miles. He turned it loose and walked out of the alley carrying the shotgun over his shoulder, on the scout for another horse to steal. Whoever he pointed the scattergun at wouldn't know it wasn't loaded and would be a fool to take the chance it wasn't, the way he figured.

He wished he had a dime for a cold beer and a sandwich, but he'd spent his last dollar for the telegraph. Well, that was where he was smart, to carry that empty shotgun, he told himself. It was all about taking risks now; he told himself he had nothing left to lose.

But goddamn, he was weary of running, of being chased, of all the bad stuff and none of the good. And the pox he'd caught from the whore didn't help his disposition any either.

He cracked the scattergun open again, hoping somehow, magically, two shells would appear. But the chambers were still empty. He snapped it shut again and stood there on the sidewalk in front of a closed millinery shop, trying to decide his next play.

A bank stood across the street, but it was closed as well, the last of the dying sun reflected in its plate glass windows. ARIZONA BANK & TRUST was lettered in gold leaf. He thought of all that money that must be in that bank, and he thought of his empty pockets and nothing standing between him and riches except twelve inches of brick wall and probably that much of steel where the money was no doubt kept in a vault.

Well shit, he told himself.

He figured to rob someone since there was no store or bank open to rob. First man who came up the walk looked like he had a few bucks was who he'd rob. The problem was, it was the supper hour and most folks were either home eating supper with their families or in the saloons drinking their supper. He was glad he wouldn't have to kill anybody, and in that way the empty shotgun was a blessing.

It was a wild-assed idea, but he even thought if he could steal enough money, he could hire some gunslingers to ride with him back down across the border and break Sam out of jail and thus save face all around.

But shit, that was like asking for the moon.

He leaned against the wall of the millinery and waited as the shadows closed in around him. Now he held the shotgun down along the side of his leg so it wouldn't be so obvious. Somebody come up, he'd just raise it and point it and ask for their wallet. He had his eye on a little paint tied up down the street in front of one of the saloons. Mustang, it looked like. Nice little horse.

How long he stood there waiting he couldn't say, but the lights began to come on in the saloons up and down both sides of the street, and somewhere far off he could hear the rumble of thunder. It was almost as if he could taste the air, the way it tastes when it has rain in it, or about to come.

A stiff wind blew along the street kicking up dust, and some cowboys rode in off to the right of where he was standing, four or five of them in a bunch, and tied off up the street and went into that particular saloon, laughing and talking loud.

He realized it was Friday. First time he'd thought about the day because ever since him and Sam had left home, time didn't mean nothing to them. They didn't have to be anywhere at any particular time and had no use for watches or calendars. Time simply became lost to them.

But if he remembered correctly, it had to be Friday. Or maybe it was Saturday. He closed his eyes and saw the General bringing down the strap, felt the sting, the way it stung like when you got cut by a knife.

The anger and hatred welled in him suddenly and he didn't give a shit what he had to do, he was going to rob somebody, and if they put up a fight, well, too bad for them.

Then he heard the clomp of boots on the boardwalk coming from his left. A tall man wearing a frock coat with his trouser legs tucked down inside the tops of his boots, whistling softly to himself. Billy gripped the shotgun tight, hoped his ruse would work.

And when he stepped from the shadows, shotgun coming up in both hands, he faced the barrel of a pistol inches from his nose.

"I don't know what you're intending, son. But you look way too young to die like this," the man said. Then showed Billy his city marshal badge pinned to the backside of his lapel when he flipped it over.

"Now set that shotgun down easy or this could be the last thing you're going to see—the dark hole of my pistol barrel."

Billy swallowed hard and let the shotgun slip from his grip till it clattered to the boardwalk.

"Now put your hands where I can see them plain," the man said. "I'd not want to get caught by surprise at some little gun you might have hidden up your sleeve."

Billy raised his hands, and the lawman told him to turn and face the wall and not move because "I've got a slight case of the palsy, and this Colt has a hair trigger, and I'd sure hate to blow your brains out if I didn't have to."

Billy felt the lawman patting down his pockets and down the inside of his legs and into his boots looking for a gun or a knife. And when he was satisfied, the lawman said, "Now just march down the street ahead of me till I tell you to stop."

Billy did as directed, and soon enough he was

sitting in another jail cell, this one only slightly better than the one in Mexico.

The lawman, once he'd turned the lock, stepped back and said, "You ain't a local, so what I need to know is where'd you come from and what are you doing here?"

Billy told him what had happened.

"So you killed this daughter of a Ruales general, is that what you're telling me?" the man said.

"No sir, we didn't, but I said I did so I could hopefully save my kid brother from getting shot, figuring if they thought it was just me who did it, they wouldn't hurt Sam. But we didn't do nothing but try and save her life, and that's what thanks we got for it."

And when Billy told him the rest, how he'd wired his ma to try and get his granddaddy to come down with a company of Texas Rangers and said who his granddaddy was, the man offered a crooked smile and said, "Jesus, boy, I know your old granddaddy. You are one lucky peckerwood to be landed in my jail, and luckier still I didn't leave your brain matter splattered all over Mrs. Thurgood's hat shop. She'd hated like hell to have to wash up such a mess and who can blame her. Where's old Gus living these days?"

"Eagle Pass, the last I heard."

"You hungry, kid?"

"Enough to eat a damn dog."

"Well, we got plenty running around here."

"I know it."

"I'll be back in a little while."

Billy watched the lawman go out. He was an old bastard for doing law-dog, Billy thought. Old but way out in front of trouble, it sure seemed like. He had pulled his pistol without Billy even seeing it, and in a heartbeat too.

Then the fellow returned in a little while with a plate of food and slid it in under the door of the cell, and went and got Billy's stolen shotgun and broke it open and saw it wasn't even loaded.

He came carrying it to the cell door and held it up and said, "Jesus, boy, you must have yourself a real death wish."

"I reckon I must," Billy said, eating hungrily.

Chapter Fourteen

Billy was lying there on the cot, his arm flung over his eyes, his body aching like a fever from the whipping he'd taken at the hands of the General. *What right did that son of a bitchin' Mescan have to whip us?* He lay there seething, which did not help his physical condition any. He thought about Sam, wondered if maybe they'd taken him out and shot him by now, figuring that they'd not risk letting another escape their puny jail. He fretted over Sam terribly. His own guilt was like a sharp rock in his belly. He slept that night with a headful of bad dreams, of seeing Sam hanging from a tree, of the stabbed girl laughing at them, of his flesh being chewed by dogs.

He awoke to a stream of morning light angling in through the barred window above his head. Then heard the door to the jail open and the clomp of boots. It was the old lawman bringing him another tray of food, covered with a cheese-cloth to keep the flies off. Ira slid the tray under the door and stood back and watched Billy eat.

Goddamn but it tasted good, a thick slice of fried ham, fried potatoes, two corn dodgers, and a scoop of applesauce.

"My missus fixed it," the lawman said, retrieving a chair from the outer room and bringing it back to sit outside Billy's cell. He took out his makings and rolled him a handmade, and struck a match head off his belt buckle and held it to the tip of his shuck, then snapped it out. The smoke smelled good and reminded Billy of better times, like when Jardine would smoke in the evening on the porch of his mama's house, and him and Sam would sit at Jardine's feet there on the steps and listen to Jardine tell stories about all what he did in his life.

"Thank your missus for me, would you?" Billy said when he finished the plate.

"I'll do it," the lawman said. "I wired your grand-daddy, told him I had you in the jail down here. I reckon I'll get an answer back from him pretty quick if he's still alive. You know if he's still alive?"

Billy shrugged. In truth, he did not know if Gus was still alive. He could only hope that he was.

"From what I know about him, I'd say he's too tough to be dead. Hell's bells, I figure he cares anything about us he's already on his way with a passel of Rangers," Billy said bravely.

The lawman looked at him askance through a veil of his cigarette smoke.

"I know those Rangers is some bad sons a bitches," Ira said, "but even they wouldn't cross that river and go into Mexico. It'd start another damn war if they did."

Billy suddenly felt glum.

"You don't know him then," he said defiantly. "I mean he whipped the Comanches all up and down Texas every which away. He sure as hell can whip a few of them damn Mescans."

"Hell, I know old Gus Rogers is bad on miscreants and such," Ira said. "He arrested me once and put me in prison. Hadn't been for his hard ways, I'd probably be dead my own self right now. He prayed with me to turn my life around before they took me off to the jail and I'll never forget him for that."

It was something Billy didn't know about his granddaddy, that he was a praying man. But then there were a lot of things he didn't know about his granddaddy because his mama had moved them away every time she got up with some man or another, and only occasionally did the Cap'n drive to wherever it was they were living at the time and see them. One Christmas he brought presents, and another time he stayed a week and took Billy and Sam fishing and they caught a catfish the size of a man's leg out of a muddy river. But that was about all he knew about Cap'n Rogers directly; the rest of his granddaddy's history was learned from Billy's mother when-ever she felt in the mood to talk about him. Now Billy wished he'd learned him better.

"He might just do that very thing," Billy said, trying hard to raise his own hope. "Come all the way down here and bust Sam out of the jail."

"Might grow wings and fly with the angels too, boy," the lawman said. "You play checkers?"

Billy thought of it more as an opportunity than simply passing time. Figured he might find a chance to distract the lawman and get hold of his gun or some such.

"Like a son of a bitch," Billy said.

"All right then, I'll go get the set."

Billy and Ira played nine games straight and Ira whipped him like a rented mule and said,

"It's a good thing we're not playing for money or you'd be broke as old Aunt Hattie."

"I *am* broke as old Aunt Hattie," Billy said.

"They skinned you in every way a man could get skinned down there, didn't they?"

"Worse than you can know."

"I'll have the doctor come and look at you soon as he gets back from the Johnson place. Mrs. Johnson's about to have her eighth child and Doc's been out there all night waiting on it."

"I appreciate it if he was to come and give me something for these whip marks."

"You want to go again?"

Billy saw there was no opportunity to reach through the bars and grab the lawman's gun since Ira wasn't wearing one. He'd obviously left his pistol in the outer room.

"No, I guess not," Billy said. "You've already whipped me so bad, I don't see as how there'd ever be any pleasure in it for either one of us."

"It's the only game I know," Ira said. Then he stood and folded the checkerboard after putting the checkers in a wood box with a sliding lid. He carried them out and returned with a wool blanket and handed it to Billy through the bars.

" 'Case you get cold during the night, otherwise you can fold it and use it for a pillow," he said and went out again, and Billy could hear him locking the front door after he went out. Then it was just silence.

He lay upon the cot and stared at nothing, trying hard to think how he was going to break jail again. It was break jail or face the consequences once old Gus Rogers showed up—if he showed up. He was sure if Gus thought he'd killed and raped that General's daughter, his granddaddy wouldn't take any mercy on him. From what little he recalled of Gus's nature, he was a stern man when it came to serving the law. *Well, maybe I could convince him the truth of it,* he thought, lying there in the growing heat.

He closed his eyes, and when he opened them again the lawman was standing there with another man wearing pince-nez glasses pinched on the bridge of his nose. A sleepy-looking little man with a bald head holding a black leather bag in one hand.

"This your victim?" the man said to the lawman.

"It is. Boy says they whipped him with a razor strap—some Ruales down in Old Mexico."

"Razor strap? That right, boy, they whip you with a razor strap?"

Billy nodded.

"Like I was a goddamn dog that ate off their plates," he said.

"Well let's have a look," the man said. "I'm Doctor Bunyon, and all you're about to find in this town that passes for a medico. I also cut hair and embalm if you ever find yourself in need of such services."

He nodded to the lawman, who unlocked the cell door and let him stroll in like he was visiting a sick aunt in an infirmary.

"Take off your shirt," the doctor said.

Billy did as ordered, feeling ashamed to have to let people know he'd been whipped like that. Told himself a real man wouldn't have allowed it.

The doctor touched the welts with delicate fingers, but it still hurt like the blazes while he was probing and prodding. He reached into his bag and took out a jar of something and unscrewed the lid.

"This is some healing ointment," he said. "Dab some on you every little while like this," and showed Billy how much to slather on. "Don't get it into your eyes," he said. The ointment had a distinct smell to it and even caused Billy's eyes to water a little bit.

The doctor looked at the lawman and said, "I don't find no broken ribs or nothing. He'll heal but he'll have some scars to show the ladies."

Then he stepped out of the cell, and Ira closed it again and locked it and thanked the doctor, saying how he'd walk with him up the street to the cafe where they could get some coffee. " 'Cause what I cook ain't worth drinking," Ira said.

Billy put the ointment on his cuts and welts, and it cooled the places it touched. He was grateful for any little relief.

Later the lawman came back with yet another

plate of food, announcing, "Lunch," and set it under the jail cell door where Billy could get it.

"I'll go over to the telegrapher's and check and see if your granddaddy sent a wire back yet," Ira said. "You drink coffee?"

"Yes sir, I do."

"I'll bring you back a cup."

"Thank you."

The lawman reminded Billy of Jardine a little with his easy manner. *I'm sure going to hate it if I have to shoot him,* Billy thought as he sat on the side of the cot and ate his lunch, a liverwurst sandwich with a slice of onion. *But I got to do what I got to do.*

Chapter Fifteen

JIM & THE CAP'N

We made Finger Bone midmorning. The dead men, the fire, the near to coming to being assassinated in the middle of the night was still playing in the back of my mind. How many others did those two murder and bury somewhere was the question the Cap'n asked and the one I asked myself as well. It was a question I came to conclude that would never find an answer. But I told the Cap'n we ought to mention the attack to his friend Ira Hayes, the lawman in Finger Bone, just in case he knew of anyone missing lately—it might give a clue as to what had happened to them.

"You're right, Jim. Could be all sorts of folks them two killed and buried somewhere."

His voice was near a rasp by now, and I could tell his flame was burning out sure as anything. I pretty well figured too that once he killed his own grandson, that would just about finish him, that he'd never make the trip back to Texas, much less on down to Old Mexico to retrieve his other grandson from the General. I doubted that boy was even alive.

Finger Bone would prove to be a typical little desert town: dusty and not much to it, but the sort of place that attracted bad men on the dodge from the law from either side of the border that lay just south toward the river. It was a place where the saloons outnumbered the churches ten to one and where the indecent women ruled the roost, because not many decent women would so much as hit the town limits before turning round and heading back to wherever it was they'd come from. It was also a town of men, mostly, and a handful of whores who kept them from going completely crazy. I'd ridden into a dozen such towns before, back when I was a Ranger and otherwise. They were towns that often would spring up because of a silver or gold strike or a railroad spur. And for a while, the town would beat like a young heart for a few years until the gold or silver played out, or the railroad stopped coming.

Then such towns would die a slow hard death, like a man gut shot, and be forgotten except by those who'd once been there and raised a little hell.

It was the bottom of the barrel for a lawman, the last stop before the grave, or worse, clerking in a store. I'd never met Ira Hayes, but I felt as though I already knew him because of what all the Cap'n had told me about him. My gut started to tighten the minute we entered onto the main drag because I knew that probably within the hour, I'd have to witness a killing that, no matter how you sliced it, didn't have any good to it. Killing never does, but this was going to turn out awful.

We were just coming up the drag when we heard the blare of trumpets.

"Sounds like a welcoming committee," Cap'n said.

"No, Cap'n, that sounds like funeral music to me," I said.

Then we looked on ahead and saw a black hearse pulled by a pair of Percherons followed by a bunch of people walking or riding horses or in gigs: men in bowlers and a few women in black dresses carrying umbrellas to shield against the sun. Behind the mourners was a brass band, their instruments catching the sun's glare, and a fellow beating a big bass drum slow and steady.

"Somebody sure enough is dead and getting buried this fine day," Cap'n said. The sky was as blue as a painting I once saw of the Pacific Ocean hanging in a whorehouse in Northfield, Minnesota.

"There shouldn't never be no funeral without rain," Cap'n said. "God's tears is what rain is."

I couldn't disagree. We were at a slow walk ourselves with the funeral procession a hundred or so yards ahead of us. The Cap'n took off his hat and held it to his chest, and I could see him mumbling what I supposed was a prayer and wished I was somehow better at it myself, but just dropped my eyes away out of respect.

We reined in at the saloon next to the building marked JAIL. There was black bunting in many of the storefront windows, including both the saloon and the jail.

"Must have been somebody important," I said.

"Must have been," the Cap'n said and climbed down out of his buggy with a grimace. He stood for a second getting himself back in order and I pretended not to notice. I knew his blood must be ticking in his wrist like a cheap railroad watch winding down, close as we were now to taking charge of his grandson Billy.

He turned the handle on the jail door's office but

it was locked. Cap'n offered me a troubled look.

"Let's go next door," he said, "and get us something to swallow down this road dust and find out where old Ira Hayes is."

We entered the saloon through the batwing doors, and the place was virtually empty, except for one man behind the bar reading a newspaper held up to the dim light falling through a window there at the back wall.

He looked up when we entered and folded his paper and set it atop the bar before coming down to wait on us.

"Gents," he said. He was a smallish man with handlebar mustaches and garters on the sleeves of his red shirt. "What'll it be?"

"Whiskey with a beer back," Cap'n said. "And could you kindly tell us where I might find city marshal Ira Hayes? I've come to see him on some important business."

The man paused in his reaching for a bottle on the shelf behind him, all three of us framed like a photograph in the back bar mirror.

"I'm afraid you're a little too late if you're here to conduct business with Marshal Hayes," he said, turning slow and pouring the shot glasses he'd set on the bar full to the brim with whiskey, so full you'd have to lift it gentle not to spill any.

"How's so?" Cap'n said.

"Marshal's been kilt. They're hauling him up to the boneyard now. Surprised you didn't hear what passes for a town's band playing his dirge. They just went by here couple of minutes ago. Would have gone myself, but he was no friend of mine."

"Who *kilt* him," Cap'n said. His voice was low now, tired as I'd ever heard it. I knew what he was thinking and wishing against—that it wasn't Billy that killed Ira.

"Kid he had locked up in his jail is who kilt him," the barkeep said, pulling the porcelain tap handle to fill our beer glasses, then slicing off the heads with a wood paddle before setting them before us.

Cap'n took off his Stetson and set it on the bar and rubbed his scalp, then tossed back his whiskey before setting his hat back down on his head again.

"How and when did this happen?"

"Yesterday evening," the man said, pouring himself a shot of the forty rod and tossing it back. "It's kinda early for me to be drinking but what the hell."

"You didn't say how it happened and I'll ask you again," Cap'n said.

The barkeep looked from him to me, then back at him. There was an element of danger in the Cap'n's voice when he grew irritated with someone, and the way the barkeep was casually talking about the death of Ira Hayes, I'm sure was irritating him more than just a little.

"Shit, nobody knows," the barkeep said,

shrugging his shoulders. "Somehow the kid got hold of a gun and shot him, right there inside the jail. Then he run out and stole the first horse he come to—Charlie Kilabrew's fine gray racer it was—and rode out of here like his heels was on fire."

"Which direction?"

"South," the man said.

The Cap'n stood there, tired eyes ablaze with disappointment and maybe a mixture of relief that he didn't have to kill his grandson this hour. I was still wondering how he was going to do it when the time came.

"What lays south?" the Cap'n said. "Between here and the border as far as towns go?"

The barman thought for a moment.

"Just some little crap heap don't have nothing there except for a dugout run by Terrible Donny Dixon, who sells whiskey he pisses in and unbranded horses that are to say the least suspect as to their prior ownership. He also rents cots to men equally suspect, bordermen and others whose faces adorn wanted posters; they take quite well to Terrible Donny's place. Plus he keeps a couple of fevered whores whenever he can get them. Heard you can buy you a piece of beaver for little as fifty cents, you get there on the right day."

"That's it?" Cap'n said. "The only thing between here and the river, this man's dugout?"

The man nodded. "Far as I know, unless

someone's come and built a metropolis since I was last there."

"What you want to do?" I said.

The Cap'n coughed and said, "What the hell do you think I want to do?"

He put a dollar on the bar for the refreshments, then said, "You got a telegraph in this burg?"

"Out the door and up the street, three doors down on your left."

We walked out into the sunlight again, the glare of it causing us to squint.

"I'm a son of a buck," Cap'n said, shaking his head. "That grandson of mine has turned feral . . ."

"I guess if he thought he was going to hang," I said, "it made him a desperate man, like it would any of us, you and me included."

"That boy would have had a father, or if I'd taken over that role, none of this would have ever happened."

"You can't blame yourself. You can't say one hundred percent certain either it wouldn't have happened. You remember that Forbes boy who killed his whole family? He was, what, all of fifteen? His daddy was a banker, his mama a schoolteacher. They were as good a folks as you're likely to find, living in that nice house in Houston, money in the bank. Well, he had a daddy and a mama too and everything a kid could want, and he still murdered them in their beds. And you remember how when we caught him in

Ulvalde, he wasn't sorry one bit for it. Went to his hanging with a smile on his face. Some are just born with bad blood in 'em, Cap'n. Maybe that's the way Billy is."

He turned to me then and said, "That's the longest damn speech I ever heard you give, Jim."

"I know it."

We found the telegrapher's and went in, and Cap'n had him send a telegraph to his daughter, reassuring her everything was going well.

"I hate having to lie to her," he said when we walked out again. "But I don't want her worrying herself sick over this business."

"What about afterward?" I said. "If you get Sam back. She'll have to learn about Billy then, what happened down here."

He leveled his gaze at me and said, "I don't think I'm ever going to make it back to Texas, leastways not alive, so I'll not concern myself about the consequences . . ."

"Why do you think he headed south and not north?" I said. "After what happened."

Cap'n shook his head.

"There's not a thing I know about that boy except that at one time he was sweet with blond hair and loved to fish." Then he added, "We best get going, see if we can catch up to him before something else bad happens. This whole thing is turning into a nightmare, Jim. Just a damn nightmare."

141

"You don't look fit to even ride," I said.

"I'm here to tell you, it's not the easiest thing I ever done and it's plumb wore me out to come this far, but unless I'm dead, I got to catch Billy and put him down and all the rest of what the General wants me to do to get Sam back."

I saw a sign across the street in a small plate glass window that read: DOC BUNYON, PHYSICIAN, UNDERTAKER, BARBER.

"Let's take a walk across the street if you're up to it," I said.

Cap'n saw what I was looking at.

"You think I'm that far gone, I need embalming?"

"No sir, but you could stand you something a little more potent than that cheap whiskey you been guzzling."

We entered the door, and it set off a little tinkle bell. The place had a strange odor to it like nothing I ever smelled before, a combination of hair oil and camphor. A man came out from the back with his shirt sleeves rolled up. The room we stood in had a barber's chair with a fancy steel footrest, leather seat, and porcelain arms. There was a small shelf of bottles and a mirror behind it. There were three chairs along the opposite wall with some old issues of the *Police Gazette* and a couple of DeWitt's dime novels lying on one of the chairs. Sunlight streamed in through the plate glass and lay in a patch on

142

the floor that had tufts of hair around the chair.

"You boys need a haircut or a burying?" the man said with an affable smile that reminded me of a man whose daughter I had once courted in Amarillo. His eyes settled on the Cap'n.

"You look ailing," he said.

"I am," the Cap'n said. "Damn fine observation, but then that's your job, ain't it—to tell the sick from the dead?"

" 'Tis," the man said without any indication of affront from the Cap'n's reply. "And you are in need of something that will not cure you but make the unpleasantness go away slightly, am I correct?"

"You are."

"I'd need to know what ails you in order to prescribe?"

"Cancer, if you must know," the Cap'n said. "At least according to those Texas medicos I've seen. Got it of the stomach."

"Sorry to hear. What troubles you the most, the pain or nausea?"

"Both, but mostly the pain. I got no appetite and can't sleep but a little at a time. Just wore out is all."

The man nodded, and you couldn't tell whether he was contemplating the Cap'n's situation or measuring him for a coffin.

"Just a moment," he said and went into the backroom whence he'd come and returned again

143

in a matter of moments with an amber bottle in his hand. He held it forth to the Cap'n.

"What is it?"

"Laudanum. The only thing I have to help you. It won't cure anything, but it will help with the nausea and the pain. And if you take enough of it, it will put you out like a candle flame in the wind. It will make everything seem less important."

The Cap'n hesitated taking it.

"I need to be in my right head. There's something important I've yet to do."

The physician seemed resigned and lowered the bottle.

"Well, your choice, sir."

"How much is it?" I said.

"Three dollars."

"I'll take it," I said.

"It will turn a healthy man into a dope fiend," he said by way of warning.

"I'll take my chances."

I dug out the money and handed it to him and put the bottle into my back pocket.

The Cap'n waited until we were outside before saying, "What the hell you going to do with that?"

"Take it along with us just in case."

"Just in case what?"

"You change your mind."

"I won't."

"Well, we'll have it along just in case."

He shook his head and we crossed the street again to where our animals were, and he climbed up into his hack with grit and took up the reins and snapped them. I put the bottle into my saddle pouch and climbed aboard the stud and followed along with him down the south road and the unknown, and all the while, I'm sure, even though neither of us talked about it, we were both thinking the same thing: how it was going to be once we caught Billy, and the Cap'n had to put a bullet in him.

Chapter Sixteen

BILLY

The gun had gone off as they struggled for it. Billy said how he had to use the privy; it had worked before. Ira Hayes knew his own boy would have been about Billy's age had he lived from child-birth. But he hadn't. The doctor came out wiping his hands on a towel, his face hangdog, that blustery night so many years before with the wind slashing across the Kansas prairies like sharpened knives that wanted to cut everything in their path, a hard snow ahead of it that rattled the windows till they came near to breaking.

"I did what I could, Ira, but your baby boy came out of the womb lifeless. Tried to breathe air into its nostrils, but to no avail. Stillborn is the medical term, but tragedy is the human one."

Ira and his wife were always careful after that not to try and make another one. His wife was fragile as a wildflower.

"You think we should?" she said that first night months afterward, knowing he was lonely and she was too; the two of them lying there in the dark listening to the last of the winter winds crying as if the winter was trying to stop the land from being born again.

But already fresh grass stems were struggling from the rich earth. Nature, an unstoppable force.

He'd shrugged, full of doubt whether he was too old to make a child with her, whether she was too old. The doctor had said one more miscarriage could take her too. Ira didn't want to run the risk of losing the only woman he'd ever come to love. They had named their unborn William.

"I reckon we should wait," he said. And so they had waited all through the spring and into the middle of summer. Then one day they were out cutting sod together to repair that same west wall the winter had nearly battered down, and it came a sudden rainstorm. The sky darkened the color of ripe plums and the air seemed to shimmer with something uncertain and became very still for a time. Blackbirds hurried away from the storm's approach, winging their way across the sky. They could see lightning like twisted wire dancing in the distance. Ira remembered an abandoned bachelor's one-room soddy within a mile of where they were and rushed her into the wagon and whipped the team of horses with a fury. They arrived just as the first raindrops the size of liberty dollars began hammering down.

They huddled inside under a smidgen of roof rafters that still had some sod on them, and the storm quickly surrounded them with a roar and a fury that wasn't uncommon on the plains. At times the ground shook from the thunder and she clung to him, afraid, and he held her, unafraid, even though he'd seen what a storm like that could do to beasts and humans. He'd once been a drover on the long trails out of Texas when he was just a kid and had seen men and cattle killed dead by lightning. He had seen dry washes and gullies suddenly roaring with a wall of water that would and could drown a cowboy looking for strays. But he was unafraid, because he was a man who believed firmly in the fates—that if it was your time to go, you were going to go, and not heaven nor hell nor all the gods, Christian or otherwise, could prevent your going. He believed, and he told her this one time while they were courting, that a man's days are numbered in the book of life, and when your number comes up, that's it.

She'd said to him at that time, "Are you a Christian, Ira?"

"No ma'am, I don't reckon so." (This before he met Cap'n Rogers, who'd arrested him and prayed with him till he felt born again.)

"That's too bad," she'd said. "I was raised to believe in Jesus and the Holy Bible."

"I hope it don't change things with us," he said.

"No, I don't suspect it will. You can't always help who it is you fall in love with, can you?"

"No ma'am."

So there they were now cleaved to one another with the rain coming in and her trembling in his arms and as sudden as a lightning bolt his desire for her flashed within him. The next they knew they were being intimate there on the ground of that old bachelor's hut, the rain falling in around them, the mighty sky dark and brooding, the ground trembling, and she kept saying, "We must be careful, Ira. We must."

"Yes, yes," he said. And he tried his best to be careful, but neither of them was sure afterward if he had been careful enough. Then the late fall arrived and trouble arose within her pert body. The baby she carried because he was not careful with her wanted to come early. He remembered blood and water on the floor. He remembered her cries of agony as they waited for a doctor who never arrived. He remembered burying her in the same ground they'd used for a garden when it was planting time. He remembered how alone he felt and all the rest till he went way wrong in life and became what he became—an outlaw of sorts. Then fate brought him Cap'n Rogers, and it all got better after he stepped out of the prison gates.

He was thinking about all these things that evening as he sat playing checkers with Billy, how he'd have liked a son with her, and mourning the loss of his wife and the two babies she nearly had, both boys as it turned out. Then Billy suddenly said, "I sure got to use that privy, Mr. Hayes."

Ira didn't see much caution in it. The boy was soft-spoken and respectful enough, and besides, he'd go and get his pistol and strap it on, and nobody but a crazy person who was unarmed would try a man wearing a gun.

Ira walked him out back and waited outside the shithouse door studying the night sky laced with stars like the sequins on a gown of a songstress he'd seen one time at the Birdcage Saloon in Tucson. And as much as he reflected on the sorrows of his life, he was grateful for what he presently had, a good new wife and a baby on the way, a decent job, and a little money in the bank. He thought himself a lucky fellow.

He was leaning there looking up at the sky when Billy suddenly burst out and grabbed hold of him quick as anything Ira could have anticipated. His fatal mistake: forgetting how old he'd become and how slow his reflexes compared to those of a wild youth.

They struggled for the gun and Billy wrested it from his grip finally, and aimed it cocked at him and said, "Don't make this harder than it has to be, Mr. Hayes. I don't want to shoot you." Then Billy marched him back inside the jail.

"Just undo these manacles round my wrists and let me go and you'll be home this night safe in bed with your wife."

"There sure is nothing I'd like more, son."

Billy had the revolver aimed at Ira's chest as he used the key to unlock the manacles. And maybe Ira just didn't think Billy would shoot him. He knew if he let a prisoner escape, the city council would probably fire him, say he was too old for the job. Incompetent. If it hadn't been for the letter of recommendation from Cap'n Rogers, he might never have gotten the job in the first place. He sure didn't want to lose it, he told himself. He had Jane to worry about as well. Jobs were scarce as it was. He could wait and see what was to happen and let fate take its course, as he'd always done. But maybe this was one time where he had to take a hand in it. And as he stared down the barrel of his own pistol, he decided fate was dictating he take action.

He made his play, and Billy pulled the trigger, and Ira dropped back like somebody had clubbed him. He fell to the floor groaning.

Billy shucked off the remaining manacle and bent over the fatally wounded man and looked him in the eyes.

"Why'd you do it, Mr. Hayes? You could have just gone on and let me leave out of here and you'd be . . ."

"Jesus," Ira muttered and reached his hand forth to Billy, who thought he was saying an epithet but quickly realized he thought Billy was Jesus. Billy backed away, just out of reach of Ira's trembling fingers. "Jesus, where's Katherine?" Ira said in a voice so low and soft, Billy barely could make out the words. "Didn't she come with you?" Billy knew from Ira's having spoken of her that Katherine was Ira's first wife, the one who lost the babies and died in childbirth.

Billy stood away, tucked the revolver into his belt, and ran out the door. There were half a dozen saddle horses tied up in front of Avery's Wild West Billiard Emporium & Oyster Bar, and Billy jumped the first one he came to and rode off into the dark just as several men came out talking loud and laughing. The men were cowboys off a nearby cattle outfit, and when they saw one of their horses had been stolen they gave chase but lost the villain in the darkness, and returned to learn that the sheriff had been murdered by his boy prisoner. It was what everyone talked about the rest of that night in every saloon, the killing of old Ira Hayes.

Doc Bunyon came and got the body with the help of his retarded assistant, Olaf, and laid Ira on a table fashioned from an old wood door with the knobs removed and set on a pair of sawhorses. Drained him of his blood and fluids using an embalming machine he bought off an army surgeon who'd used it in the Civil War, a dandy little machine made of copper and rubber tubes. He then sent the retard to Ira's house to ask the widow Hayes to pick out a suit of clothes. The town preacher had been notified of the killing and had gone straight to Ira's house and informed Jane Hayes of the tragic events and sat with her for comfort's sake. It was the preacher who answered the door when Olaf knocked and stated his reason. Jane Hayes was too distraught, and so the preacher told Olaf to go and pick from the closet what he needed. The retard came back with black coat and checkered trousers and a blue shirt.

"What about the shoes?" Doc Bunyon wanted to know, and the retard started back to get shoes but Doc said, "Never mind, he don't need shoes where he's going." Then he trimmed Ira's hair around his ears and combed the rest down with rose water, parting down the middle with a rubber comb. He finished the task by waxing Ira's gunfighter mustaches, and powdered his cheeks.

"How's he look?" he asked the retard.

"Pretty," the retard said.

Chapter Seventeen

JIM & THE CAP'N

We'd not gone a mile from Finger Bone when the Cap'n slumped over in the hack. I rode alongside and grabbed the reins and brought it to a halt.

"Cap'n!"

His eyes rolled my direction but I could see he was in a terrible way. A grove of cottonwoods stood just off the road and I led the hack over there, then lifted the Cap'n out and laid him under the shade. I got the laudanum out of my saddle pouch and told him to take a swallow. He tried waving it off, but I insisted, and he finally took a long swallow of it, then lay back and closed his eyes. I wondered if this was it, if the Cap'n's string had run out.

He lay there for a few moments, then opened his eyes again.

"I'm sorry, Jim . . ."

"Nothing to be sorry for," I said.

"Maybe this dope the doctor give me will take hold in a few minutes and I'll be able to go on."

153

"I'm going to take you back to Finger Bone," I said.

He shook his head.

"No, I need to go find Billy before it's too late." He cringed, then took a deep breath and let it out again. "Maybe I could stand another swallow of that." I put the bottle of laudanum to his mouth and he drank. And after a few minutes he said, "That's helping some."

I waited another half an hour, then said, "What do you think?"

He shook his head.

"I'm not sure I'm able to move just yet."

"I've got an idea," I said.

"I'm listening."

"I'll take you back to Finger Bone and let you rest up there, and I'll go on ahead and see if I can find Billy. I'll ride to that dugout on the river and see if he's there. How will that suit you?"

He slowly nodded his head.

"Maybe it's best," he said. "I sure hate to leave this on you, Jim."

"You're not leaving anything on me I didn't want put on me," I said. "That was the case, I wouldn't be here now." I helped him up into the hack, tied the stud on back, and rode him back to Finger Bone. I got him a room at the hotel and got him into it.

"I'll be back in a day one way or the other. If

not, you know something didn't go right. Otherwise, I'll see you back here tomorrow."

By late afternoon, along toward dusk, I came to the dugout the barkeep back in Finger Bone told us about. Just beyond it ran the river, glittering like broken glass with the last of the sun in it.

There were three saddle horses and a mule tied up out front. The dugout was long and low and had but two windows notched into the logs; one was covered in oilskin and the other had cheap glass. The doorjamb was without benefit of a door but had a heavy tarp rolled up and tied off above the frame I supposed was used instead of a door when the need arose.

One of the saddle horses was a gray, the same color the barkeep described as having been stolen.

I reined in and tied up next to the gray, then dismounted. I didn't know what the kid looked like but I'd figure it out.

I stepped in through the opening of the doorway. It was cool and dark inside, and it took time for my eyes to adjust to the poor light. Two men stood at the plank bar and one behind it. The rest of the room was in deep shadows.

I stepped to the bar and said, "Whiskey."

"Right-o," the man behind the bar said.

"You Terrible Donny Dixon?"

"Who'd be wanting to know?"

Terrible Donny Dixon had a blind eye—his left—that was the color of spoiled milk, and a long horsy face, a nose looked like it had been broken more than once, and a receding hairline with a widow's peak.

"I heard a man could buy some cheap beaver at your place," I said.

"A man could," he said.

"How much?"

"Twenty dollars, stranger. That cheap enough for you?"

I sipped the whiskey as my eyes adjusted to the dark interior of the place. There were two other men sitting at a table with a bottle between them watching me closely. They could have been on the dodge and thinking I was a lawman. Or they could have just been the curious type. My eyes scanned the room, and I saw someone sitting in the farthest corner alone, but it was too dark to tell if he was young or old. He was hatless, and I thought not many men of this country go around without a hat on.

"Too much," I said.

"How much you willing to pay?" Terrible Donny said.

"Hell, I don't know, where's the merchandise?"

He said, "Just a minute," and went around the end of the bar and over to the doorjamb and shouted, "Maize, get your goddamn ass in here!" In a few moments a thin, emaciated woman came in through the door and over to the bar, and the other men watched her like she was a prize steer they were getting ready to bid on for supper. "Fellow is looking for some beaver," Terrible Donny said. "Wanted to see the goods before he plunked down his money. Show him the goods, honey." She pulled down the top of her shift to reveal two small breasts the size of pears. Just looking at her eyes, the way they were sunk in, the dark circles under them, the sallow skin, the skinniness, you could tell she was a dope fiend and probably not more than eighteen or nineteen years old, but looked twice that if you knew anything about dope fiends.

"Think I'll pass," I said, still keeping an eye on the fellow in the corner. If he came up out of his chair I was set on shooting him and anyone else in that stinking place who might want to give me trouble. I was tired and longing for home again, and I wanted to get this business over with soon as possible.

"How about two dollars for her," Terrible Donny said. "She's worth a good two dollars."

"No," I said, "but you can tell me where your privy is."

"Out back," he said. "And that will be one dollar for the whiskey."

I paid it rather than argue and walked outside and waited around the side of the dugout to see who came out. I wanted to see who the man was sitting in the corner and if he climbed aboard the gray. I slipped my Merwin Hulbert from the shoulder holster and held it in my hand down along my leg.

One hour passed, then another, and the land started to take on the shadows of night, and I could hear the woman inside laughing at something, then heard something break, like glass. I heard Terrible Donny curse at something. His voice was distinct, nasal and high-pitched like you might think a man would talk who had had his nuts cut off. Then right after the sun set completely, throwing off the last of its light against a gunmetal sky, and buttery light fell through the two windows out into the darkness, a lone figure stepped out of the dugout and went straight for the gray.

I stepped out of the shadows and said, "Billy Rogers."

He paused, one hand on the saddle horn, staring over the back of the horse.

"You got me confused with someone, mister," he said.

"I'm here to arrest you," I said.

The horse was between us.

"No mister, you've got me confused with someone else. My name's not Billy Rogers."

"What is it then?"

He hesitated just a moment too long, enough to have to think up an alias, and I knew without a doubt it was him.

"Jardine," he said. "That's my name, Jardine Frost."

"Step away from that horse."

"No sir, I can't."

"You can go hard or you can go easy, son."

"Fuck, I don't guess I'll be going at all!"

He jerked the reins free of the hitching post and spooked the horse so that it twisted and reared, and when it did a blaze of light flashed and I felt the kid's slug go through the sleeve of my shirt between my left elbow and wrist, even as I brought up my own piece and fired back.

My first slug took his horse. It reared, then fell dead. My second slug knocked the kid down but he scrambled to his feet again and ducked into the dugout. I could hear him inside shouting at the others to back away or die. Then there was a burst of gunfire, something big—like a scattergun and two bangs from a pistol. Several men came rushing out with their hands in the air shouting, "Don't shoot! Don't shoot!"

I collared one and said, "What's happened inside?"

He stuttered that Terrible Donny had pulled his sawed-off from behind the bar aiming to kill the kid but that the kid shot him first and Terrible Donny's shotgun blast had taken off the top of the whore's head.

"Jeez Christ!" he said. "Jeez Christ! Poor Maize!"

I turned him loose, and he ran away like a frightened dog.

I ran over and jerked my Henry from its scabbard and unloaded all sixteen shots in through the windows in rapid order. I wanted the kid to know I wasn't fooling around.

"I'm here on behalf of your granddaddy, Gus Rogers," I called when the last shot's echo died. "You want to come out of there walking or feet first, it doesn't matter to me. But you ought to know Gus isn't going to save you. He's dying."

There was a long silence.

"Who you?" he said.

"Not that it matters, but my name is Jim Glass. I used to Ranger for your granddaddy."

"How I know you won't shoot me?"

"I just come to get you, kid, take you to him, is all. I've got no reason to shoot you unless you give me one."

"He come to help save Sam?"

"He did, but he's sick as hell in a town north of here a little ways."

"You said you come to arrest me, earlier."

"Arrest, get, what's the difference? You look around and tell me if there's not been enough killing here today."

"They'll just hang me if I give up," he said. "Might as well go out guns blazing."

"I don't know, kid. One way, you might stand a chance with a jury, but with me, you'll stand no chance at all. Your choice, but I'm not going to sit out here all night. I'm going to come in there and get you if I have to. I've done this sort of work before, and trust me, I'm good at it."

All the while I was reloading the Henry, not to try and kill the boy, but show him some of the effect of no-holds-barred warfare. I slipped the last round into the magazine and emptied it again into the building as fast as I could lever and shoot.

Then I waited a moment till the silence surrounded us and said, "Well, you coming out or not?"

Chapter Eighteen

Sam & the General

The Mexican general studied him till it got on his nerves. Just stood there and stared in on him.

"What you want?" Sam said, almost shyly, but with a hint of defiance too.

"You think he's coming, don't you, your famous grandfather, the Texas Ranger?"

"Yes, he's going to come and bust me out of this spit bucket."

The General sucked his teeth contemplatively.

"I think if he comes at all, he will have the head of your brother in a basket for me."

Sam felt the bite of the comment as if it had teeth.

"Tell me, was it your idea or your brother's to set upon my daughter?"

"I keep telling you we didn't do nothing but try and save her life, mister!"

"If you keep insisting you are innocent, then you leave me no choice to show you any mercy. How can I have mercy on someone so cold-blooded?"

"Did you all find a knife anywheres? Because me and Billy sure weren't carrying no knives on us. And I don't know how you could say we stabbed your girl if we didn't have no knives."

Thus far no knife had been found, and this troubled the General greatly. He was an observant man; his military training had caused him to be so. He was strategic as well.

"Tell me what you did with the knife," he said. "It might go easier on you."

Sam shook his head disconsolately.

"I don't know why you can't believe nothing," he uttered.

"You know how this is going to work?"

Sam shook his head.

"I have told your grandfather that if he will find and kill your brother, that I'll let you live."

Sam bowed his head, looked at the floor.

"I didn't do nothing. And Billy *didn't* do nothing either!"

"He confessed."

162

"Just to save me."

"Then he was a fool, it won't save you, his supposed lies. Nothing is going to save you, my young friend."

"Then why not just kill me if that's what you all are intent on doing? Why not just get it over with?"

"You must understand fully the gravity of what you've done and repent."

"Fuck, I don't even know what that means—repent."

"You are a crude young gringo."

"I reckon maybe I am, but I don't know how else to be," Sam said. "It ain't like I got much to lose at this point in the game by trying to show you my good side, now does it?"

"You think that is what this is, a game?"

"No sir."

The General thought the boy disarming in his manner: one moment talking tough like a man much older, the next shy as a schoolgirl. But he felt no compassion for him because of their crimes. Even a young snake can kill you with its poison.

"How does it feel?" the General said.

"How does what feel?"

"To suffer, to never know the hour of your death?"

Sam touched the lacerated places of his face and body where he'd been whipped.

"I guess I know a little of what old Jesus went through before they killed him," Sam said.

"You believe in Jesus?"

"I do, yes sir."

"You think he will be waiting for you in heaven?"

"Yes sir."

"You think he knows what you did to my daughter and that he will forgive you for it?"

Sam looked up, his eyes full of grief.

"He didn't see me do nothing like it. I may have done some bad things but I never did what you said."

The General slapped him across the face with an open hand so hard, the sound was like a pistol shot. It knocked Sam senseless for a moment.

"You will own to it before it is over," the General said.

"That what you want? Me to own to something I didn't do?"

The General slapped him again, just as hard, and Sam tasted the salt of his own blood as it leaked from his lips and his nose.

The General smelled of cloves, his eyes black as the beads on a woman's necklace. He just needed hooves and horns and he'd be the damn devil.

The General walked out of the cell and the Ruales guard with him locked the door.

Left alone finally, Sam felt himself shrinking inside. He tried hard not to think about what it would be like in those final minutes when they came and dragged him from the jail—for he would not go willingly—and stood him in front of a wall (wasn't that the way they did it?) and tied his hands behind his back. He tried not to think what it would be like looking down the barrels of their aimed guns and waiting for that instant when they pulled their triggers and how the bullets would feel punching into him, and if when you died did you float off this earth into heaven or was it more like just a forever blackness where you didn't think or feel anything.

Forever blackness. It broke his heart to think there might be a forever blackness.

He thought of Rebecca, their neighbor girl back home who lived in the house next to Jardine's place where his mama had moved him and Billy to be with Jardine. Rebecca had strawberry-colored hair and budding bosoms and a sweet way about her. She was a year older, and seemed several years wiser. And when she kissed him that one evening underneath the tree with the sound of cicadas buzzing all around, he thought he had never felt anything as good or would again, until she reached for his hand and put it inside the top of her dress and he felt the small, firm, rounded bosoms and the rapid beating of her heart.

Something happened to him that evening. Something in him broke like a wall pushed by too much water behind it, and he felt a warmness issuing from him and wondered if he'd wet his pants. But it was worse than that. Much worse. And it scared and embarrassed him even as the pleasurable sensation washed over him.

"Oh my," she said when she noticed as he twisted away. Then giggled into her hand saying, "No, Sam. I'm not laughing at you."

He ran off leaving her there under the tree, too embarrassed to speak, and for a week or more hid out, Billy and his ma saying, "You sick or something?"

The last time he saw her, she wanted to talk to him about it, but he begged her not to and they kissed and sat sweetly holding hands, Sam pining away for her, to touch her again like he did when he had his accident, but afraid he'd have another.

Then Jardine suddenly got himself killed and it was a mournful time till Billy said they ought to leave off out of there and strike out on their own.

Now as he sat caged and bleeding, his whole face hurting like the blazes, he pined for her, for home, for his ma, even for Jardine. And it all got worse when he thought that maybe Billy was even dead, his body lying out there somewhere, the buzzards and wolves eating it.

I come into this world with nothing, he finally told himself. *And I guess I'll go out of it with nothing.*

He could not see them because there were no windows in the jail to see them with. But he thought the stars might be falling.

166

Chapter Nineteen

JIM & BILLY

It went on like that for a while, me waiting outside the dugout for Billy to make his play—to go out in a blaze of glory as he said it, or to throw down his weapon and come out peaceful. The air buzzed with flies.

"You liking it in there with those dead people," I called at one point. "You're going to join them, you don't get your ass out here."

"I need your assurance you won't shoot me if I come out," he said.

"I already told you, kid, I'm not here to kill you. I just come to get you to your granddaddy."

Another thirty minutes ticked off, then he said, "I'm coming out!"

"Toss your piece out first," I said.

His pistol came out through the busted window and landed in the dirt. Then he appeared in the open door frame holding his shoulder, his fingers painted with blood.

"You busted my damn shoulder with one of your shots," he said, grimacing.

I told him to sit on the ground while I went inside to check on the scene. And it was as one of the patrons who'd run out earlier said it was—two dead, one a woman. I mean both god-awful dead with the flies eating their blood. There wasn't any time to bury them. I figured somebody would surely find them quick enough and do the job for me, or burn the place down around them. There just wasn't any time to waste.

I helped the kid struggle into the saddle of his horse that had run off a little ways but then stood cropping the local vegetation of grass there by the river's edge where I caught it up easy enough.

We rode north again with the rising sun off to our right painting the desert red, then golden. You could feel the heat already rising from the desert floor. A Harris hawk sat perched atop a saguaro and watched us with an alert eye as we passed down the road.

Then it suddenly took flight, went into a low glide, and snatched a packrat with its talons and lifted high into the air again, working its wings mightily, breakfast caught.

"I feel like that packrat," Billy said. "Just like it." He rode slumped to his offside where his shoulder was broke from my bullet.

"Don't die on me, kid," I said.

"Hell, why not?"

I didn't have an answer for him. And to tell the truth, maybe it wouldn't have been so bad if he had died. It would save the Cap'n the trouble of doing the deed. But still, something in me didn't want the kid to die.

We had to ride slow because of the kid's busted shoulder. But before we ever reached Finger Bone, I saw the Cap'n's hack sitting off to one side of the road, the horse still in its traces, its head down, the Cap'n slumped over in the seat.

I figured the Cap'n was dead. That he'd got up his grit to follow us and just died, and the harnessed horse finally just stopped pulling without anyone to guide it.

I reined the stud in thinking the whole journey had been a failure, remembering what I'd promised the Cap'n if he died—that I'd go down and try and save the other boy and kill the General if I had to. I sure did not want to.

The Cap'n lay on his side across the seat with his eyes closed, his hat fallen off his head.

"That him?" Billy said.

"It is."

I dismounted and told the kid to get down and he nearly fell getting off the horse because of his bad shoulder.

"Sit on that rock yonder," I said, and he went over and sat on it because he looked like he was close to fainting.

I went over and shook the Cap'n, and at first he didn't move. I shook him again and he roused, but slowly, never even reaching for his pistol, which told me he was in bad shape. I've never seen him come awake without reaching for his pistol.

"Huh . . . what is it?" he muttered.

"You okay?" I said.

He looked around till he saw Billy sitting there on the rock. His eyes narrowed. I saw the lines around his mouth tighten. The boy looked up.

"You my granddad?" he said.

Cap'n nodded.

"Come here, boy," he said.

"I can't."

Cap'n looked at me.

"What's wrong with him," he said. Then he saw the blood on the side of my shirt, dried now to a reddish brown.

"We had a problem," I said. "He didn't want to come along. His shoulder's broke from a bullet."

The Cap'n looked aggrieved.

"You been taking your medicine?" I said.

"Too much of it, it seems. I thought I had it in me to catch up with you. Didn't want to lay this whole thing on your back, Jim. Last I knew I was just driving along, and gawd almighty, I wake up and you're standing here. My head feels like it's stuffed full of cotton."

"You don't look too well."

"I don't feel too well, to be truthful with you. Had some real bad dreams."

"What do you want to do here?" I said.

"You know what I've got to do," he said.

The kid sat listening. You could tell he suspected something bad was about to happen, like a dog you're about to put down, or a horse when you approach it with your gun behind your back—they just know. The kid just knew.

"Listen," I said. "I'm going to walk off up that road just a little and leave you to your business. Then I'll come back. That okay with you?"

He nodded.

I glanced at the kid one last time, then led my horse up the road where there was a bend in it that would take me out of sight of the Cap'n and his grandson. I didn't want to see it. I knew it would be a scene that would live with me all the rest of my days if I saw it.

I walked with an ache behind my eyes and wished I had a whole bottle of whiskey to drink myself into a stupor. Maybe it would help, maybe it wouldn't. I got around the bend and stood there in the road waiting for the pistol shot that would kill the kid. I wish I didn't have ears to hear with, either.

Time seemed to stand still like the whole world was frozen in a moment. Then: BANG! A single shot. The sound quickly got swallowed by the vast desert as though it never happened. I turned around and walked back, expecting to see the last thing I wanted to see.

Only what I saw wasn't at all what I expected.

The Cap'n lay dead on the ground, his gun still

in his hand, one side of his head blown out, his boots pointed skyward, the dust soaking up his blood. Billy sat there on the rock staring at him.

"What the hell happened?" I said.

Billy shook his head.

"He shot himself," he said.

"Goddamn, I can see that, boy!"

"I thought he was going to shoot me," Billy said, his whole body trembling now. "He said he was bound to kill me in order to save Sam. He said, 'I hate to do this worse than anything, son . . .' Then he cocked his gun and I said, 'Yes sir, I understand. You got to do what you got to do. Go on and do it.' He told me to look away, that he didn't want me to look at him. I told him I wasn't going to look away. Told him that I wasn't afraid of dying as much as I was to keep living. Told him that I'd messed up my life pretty good, but if he by God was going to kill me, I wanted him to look me in the eyes when he done it.

"He said, 'Yes sir, you surely have ruined your life. I just don't know why it was you went so bad so young. I guess if I'd been there for you, you would have turned out different than you have.' I told him it wouldn't have made no difference— that I'd probably have gone bad either way, that I thought I just had bad blood in me. He said, 'Is that why you killed that woman and my friend Ira Hayes?' I told him I killed that lawman because he was going to kill me for trying to escape—that it

172

wasn't something I wanted to do, that it was an accident.

"He said, 'What about that woman, that just an accident too?' I said, 'No sir. I never did kill no woman,' and explained it all to him. You know what he said when I told him that?"

I shook my head.

"He said, 'I believe you, boy. I been around liars and cheaters and badmen all my born life and I know one when I see one. You might be a lot of things, but I don't think you're a liar.' I said, 'Well, that's it then, go ahead and pull your trigger and get this over with.' "

I waited as the kid hesitated, blinking back whatever was in his eyes.

"Then he just said, 'I'm all in, boy. I'm finished as finished can be, and I'll be damned if I'm going out with such sin on my head. So long, boy,' and turned the gun on himself before I could try and stop him . . ."

Tears began to stain the kid's dirty cheeks, his resolve to be hard-bitten was broken at last, broken in a way no bullet or threat of death could break him.

"Thing is," I said, kneeling by the Cap'n and taking the gun out of his hand, then gently closing his half-open eyelids. "He wouldn't have lasted another week. He was eat up with cancer. I guess he just couldn't do what he'd always done in the past."

The kid rubbed the tears from his eyes with the heel of his hand.

"What's that?" he said.

"His job," I said.

"Where does it stand now," he said, "between you and me?"

"If your granddaddy didn't kill you and bring your head in a basket to him, the General was going to shoot Sam, that was the deal," I said.

"Then you best go on and do it. Sam's a good boy and never done nothing truly wrong other than what I talked him into doing. He don't know much better—he's just a kid. Hell, what difference does it make to me if I'm alive or if I'm dead." He looked at his bum shoulder. "I'll never be able to use this no more and I'd as soon be dead as be a cripple anyways."

I stood away from the Cap'n's body. My old friend. I looked at the kid. I told myself I should just ride away from this, that maybe the younger boy was already dead, and even if I killed this boy and did what the General wanted, I'd just be wasting my time doing a dirty business I wouldn't ever be able to wash from my hands.

There was already too much good blood spilled as it was.

Chapter Twenty

I bent and picked up the Cap'n's body and got it into the hack.

"You think you can drive this with one arm?" I said to Billy.

He nodded.

"Then get in and take the reins."

"Where we going?"

"To Old Mexico," I said.

For the first time I saw something akin to fear in his eyes.

"They'll kill us both we go down there with no army of guns to back us," he said.

"I'm going to see if I can trade you for that kid brother of yours. That's the plan, kid."

He stiffened.

"I wish you'd just do it instead," he said. "Pull the trigger on me rather than let those dirty Mescans have at me."

"You don't always get what you want in this life," I said.

"I don't want that dirty Mescan killing me!"

"What difference does it make who does it?"

"Makes a lot to me. He whipped me like I was a damn dog. Whipped Sam too. He had no right."

"He thought you killed his daughter; you're lucky he didn't shoot you on the spot."

"I wished to hell he had."

"Wishing don't make it so, kid."

I told him to lead out and he took up the reins in his good hand and snapped them over the rump of the horse, and we splashed across the river, and I thought, *There is no turning back.* By midday we made the village of Arroyo according to the sign on a side of a livery; a sleepy little burg that stood baking under the noon sun. A collection of clapboards and adobes without a single thing I could see to recommend the place. But I was hoping we could find a doctor, though, to look at the kid's shoulder. It was one thing to take him down to Old Mexico to be murdered, another thing to let him suffer on the way. I am not by nature a cruel man, or at least I'd like to believe that I am not. And I needed to find an undertaker for the Cap'n. I wanted him to have a decent burial.

I stopped the first person I saw, a woman sweeping the front of her adobe stoop. She was fat and brown with raven black hair twisted into a cone atop her head. She wore a red blouse and dark blue skirt and sandals on her feet that were dusty. She paused when I rode up and spoke to her and asked her if the village had a doctor.

"*Qué?*"

"Medico," I said. She looked from me to the

boy, then to the tilted form of the Cap'n, and crossed herself and pointed up the street. We rode on. I saw a man, a white man, washing the windows of a cantina and asked him where the doctor was, and he turned to look at me and the kid and the body of the Cap'n.

"Across the street upstairs over the jeweler's," he said. He was wearing a big Walker Colt on his hip. I thought it must be a pretty bad town if a man had to wear a sidearm just to wash his store window.

"Who does the burying in your town?" I asked.

"The German, Hass. Digs the graves, no undertaker; he just puts them in quick, if you know what I mean, it being hot as hell down this way." Then he paused and chuckled and said, "I guess it's hot as hell in hell too, if that's where you're headed."

"Where might I find this Hass?"

"Keeps a place out at the cemetery, lives there, can't miss it. Just go on up this road to about half a mile out of town. You'll see it on your right."

I thanked him and we went across the street and I tied up the horses and helped the kid out of the wagon.

"What about him?" he said, looking at his granddaddy.

"He's not going anywhere."

I guess he saw the wisdom in that and climbed the stairs ahead of me, and we knocked on the door and it was soon opened by a thin man with dark skin and a widow's peak of silver-streaked hair and spectacles.

"Got a patient for you," I said in Spanish. "You speak gringo?" He nodded, said, "Sí. *Poquito*, a little."

"This boy's got a bullet-busted shoulder, do what you can for him, I've got money."

He had the kid remove his shirt, then examined his busted shoulder, shaking his head. "How did this happen?" the medico asked.

"That sum bitch standing yonder," Billy said, pointing at me with his nose.

I ignored the remark and rolled myself a shuck and smoked it while the doctor cleaned out the wound and wrapped it and set a sling for the boy's arm.

"I can't do much for you," he said. "I've not too much to work with here in this place. Do you use this hand or the other one?"

"This," Billy said, looking down at the hand of his wounded shoulder.

"Then you will need to learn to use the other one," the doctor said.

"How much for the services?" I said as the doctor shook some pills from a bottle into a small envelope and handed them to Billy, telling him to take them as he needed them for the pain. "Take one or two now, if you wish?" Then he said to me, "Five American dollars."

I dug around in my wallet for five dollars in paper money and handed it to him.

"We've got to go, kid," I said.

Billy stood unsteadily and we went down the stairs again, and we drove out to the cemetery, where we saw two men digging a fresh grave. We rolled up to the iron fence and I dismounted. They stopped digging as I approached.

"I got a man needs burying," I said. "A friend."

One was a large man with a barrel chest wearing a thin, sweat-soaked shirt with the sleeves rolled up past his elbows, and a beard that looked like a hawk's nest. The other man was short and dark-skinned, wiry as a terrier. His work clothes were dirty, ragged at the knees. His straw hat was busted out in the crown.

"Yah, I bury yer friend," the big man said with a German accent. "Where you have him, eh?"

"Over in that rig," I said, pointing to the hack.

"We get him for you, then," the German said, and both men laid their shovels aside and went and carried Cap'n out of the hack and laid him there on the ground near the grave they were digging.

"Head shot, eh?" the German said, looking at the Cap'n's bloody head wound.

"Yes," I said.

"Pretty bad deal for him."

"You going to bury him in that grave you're digging now?"

179

"Yah. Why not?"

I shrugged and nodded with approval. There was no reason not to bury the Cap'n as quickly as possible. No need for a funeral and no mourners except Billy and me to attend it.

"You think you can get a priest to come and say a prayer for him?" I said. The German nodded and looked at his smaller companion, who hurried off toward town.

"We dig all the time, eh. Always somebody needs buried, yah. We finish this, we start and dig two more right away. Always the same, three graves a day, more if we need to. That way we stay ahead of the work, yah."

"How much for the burial?"

"Ten dollars if you don't want no coffin, fifteen if you do."

I took out the last of my money, then realized I probably should empty the Cap'n's pockets of his possessions. I knelt and took out his effects: a wallet with close to a hundred dollars still in it, a tintype of a young woman holding an infant with a towheaded boy clinging to her skirts—Sam, I figured, was the baby and Billy the boy—a heavy pocket watch, the contents of his valise, and his fancy Russian model Smith & Wesson pistol. I stood and said, "Okay, make sure he gets the coffin and the priest prays over him."

"Yah, sure, sure. I make sure, for his soul."

Then I started to walk away. Billy was still

sitting in the hack looking stunned, and I saw he had the Cap'n's bottle of laudanum with the cap screwed off in his hand.

"Hey," the German yelled. I turned around. "What about the ring on his finger, your friend?"

He pointed. It was the Cap'n's wedding ring. I never saw him without it.

"You leave it on him," I said.

"Yah, yah, okay then."

I tied my horse on back of the hack and climbed in and took the reins from the kid and turned the hack back toward the town because we needed to eat something. My belly was rubbing my back-bone and I was tired from not having slept all night. We needed to eat and rest a little while, then hit it hard on down to the border and across.

"We turning back?" Billy said.

"Just going to town and get some grub and a day's rest. We can't go on like this, neither of us, and our horses need rest as well."

We found a livery and I paid the liveryman there to feed and water our horses while Billy and I walked up to a restaurant and bought a meal: bowls of chili with chunks of beef that made your eyes water. Coffee for me. Billy asked if they had any cold buttermilk. The waiter said no. He had big black handlebar mustaches and acted as though this was the worst work in the world for a man to be doing. Maybe it was. Billy said, "I'll have a glass of beer then if you don't mind."

When we finished we walked up the street to the one and only hotel according to the waiter. It stood on the corner across from a bank. On the opposite corners were also a hardware store and a saddle maker shop.

The clerk behind the desk at the hotel had long sideburns that came down to his jawbone and shifty eyes.

"Two rooms next to each other with locks," I said.

He asked me in Spanish how long we'd need the rooms.

"*Una noche*," I said. Just one night.

The room charge was ten dollars.

We climbed the stairs to the upper level and walked down the hall till we found room numbers nine and ten. I unlocked nine and we went in. It was just a room with a single bed, no chair, a small table with a lamp on it. Bare floor, window that looked down into the alley that ran behind it.

I opened the window to let in some air. The room was hot and dry, the wallpaper that had once been a pattern of roses and stripes was faded and here and there peeling.

"Why it's just like the queen's palace," Billy said, looking around.

"What would you know about the queen's palace?" I said.

"Shit if I know anything about it."

"You stayed in school long enough to learn to read and write?" I said.

"Some. I read about her once—Queen Victoria. Said she lived in a palace and had servants for her wolfhounds. You believe that?"

"I wouldn't know. You go ahead and get some rest," I said and went out locking the door from the outside with the key, then opening the door to my own room, which was nothing different from the kid's.

I took off my shoulder gun rig and laid it on the table, but put the pistol under my pillow, then I sat down on the edge and removed my boots and lay back. The weight of exhaustion pressed down on me like a slab of granite. The room was hot and still, but I didn't even care.

I closed my eyes, and when I did I fell into a sweet dream about Luz.

We were swimming naked in a pool of cool water and she was laughing and we wrapped our arms and legs around each other and became like one person and made love that way, standing in the water, wrapped round each other.

I awoke sometime later in the darkness, got out of bed, and looked in on the kid, half expecting him not to be there. But he was. Sleeping in the bed just like he was a normal boy. And I wondered what he was dreaming about.

It sure couldn't be anything as pleasant as making love to a woman in water.

Chapter Twenty-One

SAM & THE GENERAL

Sam heard the mournful music outside his cell, from beyond the adobe walls. Strained and halting, it seemed like at first. Then it became less strident and uneven and more like the sad weeping of women, and he realized that it was the funeral cortege for the General's daughter. He could hear the ringing of church bells, dull and heavy with a reverberation that he could almost feel against his skin.

A Ruale stood guard outside the cell—ever since Billy had escaped. He was armed with a rifle and he did not smile or speak, for he'd been ordered not to.

"They burying the General's daughter, ain't they?" Sam said.

The Ruale's eyes flicked his way.

"Boy, that's sure enough a sad thing to hear—that dirge. She was a pretty woman," Sam said.

The Ruale looked away.

The day before, they had come and taken Sam from his cell, and he thought it was to shoot him.

They marched him down the street to a vacant lot that had an adobe wall and three wood posts set into the ground. A crowd of people had gathered and there was a line of Ruales standing there in the hot sun with their rifles. And then the old guard that had allowed Billy to escape had been brought in a wagon. He was sitting atop a coffin of white pine, it looked like. The wagon stopped and the prisoner was dragged down, his wrists and ankles in shackles. His head was cut from the beating Billy had given him, and he stood trembling as the coffin was lifted out of the wagon and carried over to the middle post. Then he was marched over to the wall where the posts were and a rope was tied around his chest to secure him to the middle post.

The General came then, riding a large black horse whose tail nearly brushed the ground. The General sat there among the gathered crowd as though allowing everyone a chance to take notice of him before dismounting. Then he went and stood among his soldiers who were lined up twenty or so paces from the prisoner. Another officer who walked along with the General handed him a cigarette already made and lighted it for him with a match.

The General smoked casually while all around him everyone stood silent, waiting. The prisoner wept openly, his whole obese body trembling. He blubbered in Spanish. Sam reckoned he was pleading for his life. Sam felt sorry for him.

Then the General motioned for the Ruales holding Sam under the arms to bring him forth and Sam thought, *Well, this is it then.* It pleased him that he had no fear of what was about to happen to him. He'd been working it through his mind for days now. Sure it was going to hurt a little, but the pain would be so quick and done with he'd only have to stand it for a mere moment. It took him longer to work through the after-dying part. He wasn't raised under the Holy Book like some. He knew a little about it, knew there was such things as heaven and hell according to the preachers. But then he thought, *I didn't know nothing before I was born so why should I know anything after I'm dead?* And he'd prayed to himself consistently ever since the Ruales had grabbed them up. But no answers or no relief came as answers to his prayers. He finally just figured either God wasn't there, or he wasn't listening if he was there.

Once he got himself settled on that point, his fear subsided.

The Ruales stood him before the General, who looked down at him with the same dead eyes he'd seen in the fish he and Billy had caught out of the river.

"You shall see now your fate," the General said. "Look at him. Like a woman he has become. Weeping and begging me for his life. You see, this is what the fear of death does to a man. It reduces him to being a baby, but only if he has enough time to think about it."

"I ain't afraid," Sam said.

The General drew deeply on his cigarette, then exhaled.

"Oh, but you will be when it comes your turn. I've seen men much braver than that one break down and weep like babies when their time has come. You don't think so now, but you'll see. To stare down the barrel of a rifle and know there is no escaping. Well, that's quite different than to just think about it. You will be like him, like a woman."

Sam figured they were going to drag him to one of those other posts and tie him up but instead they turned him around to face the prisoner, whose pleas now were more like screams.

The General nodded to his man, who gave a sharp command to the Ruales, and they brought their rifles up to their shoulders—Sam counted twelve of them. The prisoner wiggled and fought to free himself as if he were a hooked fish.

The General's man barked a second order, and the guns clattered, and Sam could see the bullets striking the prisoner, punching holes in him from which blood leaked as he sank to his knees, his head slumped, and like that he was dead.

Some of the Ruales came forward and untied the rope and then lifted him into the coffin, then another hammered shut the lid before the coffin was carried to the wagon again and carted off. Sam could see the dark stains in the dirt; they were the only evidence the guard had ever lived. Then Sam was dragged back to his cell. The whole while he repeated to himself, *I'm not afraid. I'm not afraid.*

And so now in his cell he heard the dirge of funeral music, the blare of horns, the ringing of the heavy church bells and thought, *So much death for a place so middling.*

"That's her being taken to the cemetery, ain't it?" he said to the guard.

Sam could not know that on this same day his own grandfather was being buried by a fat German less than fifty miles north.

"We didn't kill her," Sam said suddenly, more as if to convince himself than the guard. As if hearing himself say it was important to him.

The guard said nothing.

"I just want you to know that, we didn't kill her. And if you kill me, you'll be killing somebody innocent."

The guard simply blinked.

Sam sat on the side of his cot, his face in his hands.

"I ain't afraid," he muttered.

The funeral dirge went on a long time, fading slowly until there was a longing silence again.

Later that day, the General came in still in his

funeral finery; a young woman in mourning dress stood next to him. The General said, "This is one of them," to the woman, who pulled the veil away from her face. Sam could see she was much younger than the General and very beautiful as well.

She looked at him intently for a moment.

"Yes, you see how young these gringos are who come down here and commit murder on our children," the General said to her.

She came close to the bars where Sam stood and spat in his face, then turned and stalked out.

The General came very close then, his breath smelling of liquor, and Sam could tell, because he'd seen it on Jardine's face lots of times, that the General was drunk.

"You see, you have made her a mother without a child," he said. "You have just two days to live. How does it feel now? Are you still unafraid?"

"You see me crying like that fat friend of yours?"

The General offered him a sullen smirk.

"He's in heaven with his Jesus," he said. "You'll join him soon. Your grandfather, Gus, he's a man of his word. He told me he will find your brother and kill him and bring his head to me. I think he will do this. And when he does, I will kill you. Then there will be justice."

"He won't kill Billy."

"To save you? I think so that he will."

"If anybody, it will be you he'll kill."

The General reached into his fancy black coat and took out a silver flask and drank from it.

"No," he said, wiping his mouth with the edge of his hand. "He will not kill me. I will kill him if he tries. I will wipe out his bloodline. Bang, bang, bang. And bury you all three in unmarked graves."

The General used his finger as if it were the barrel of a pistol.

Sam could see that the black dye the General used on his hair and mustaches had sweated down his neck and his chin. He was an old man trying to look young, no doubt for his young wife. Sam wiped the spittle from his face. Old men and young women. Sam couldn't understand it; why a man would make such a fool of himself for a woman, why a young woman would marry an old man.

"That stuff you put in your hair," Sam said. "It's leaked all over your shirt collar."

The General motioned for the guard to unlock the cell door, then struck Sam with a winging backhand that made Sam's world go suddenly dark.

Sam's dark dreams were of fish and murder.

Chapter Twenty-Two

JIM & BILLY

"Get up," I said, tapping the soles of Billy's boots. Billy stirred and sat up painfully, guarding his busted shoulder.

It was just turning daylight outside. A slow, steady rain pecked at the window, fell in through the bottom where it was open, and wet the flooring.

"I can't feel my hand," Billy said, flexing his fingers.

"Let's go," I said. I wanted to have sympathy for the boy, but it was damn hard considering.

"I don't think I can stand the jolt of that hack," he said.

"You'll stand it or else."

"Else what?"

He was damn defiant, and it took everything in me to keep from busting him one. I took him by the good arm and helped him stand.

We went down the stairs and out the front door. Puddles of rainwater stood in the muddy street dimpled with the falling rain. The sky hung low and gray, the clouds bunched together, and there was nobody out on the streets.

191

"Let's grab some coffee and breakfast," I said, and we walked over to the restaurant and took a window seat.

"I ain't hungry," Billy said.

" 'Cause of that?" I said, pointing at his slung arm.

"I had to get up in the middle of the night and puke."

He seemed to me like a beat dog, and I felt for him the way I would a beat dog. But I'd promised the Cap'n I'd do what I could to save the life of his younger grandson even if it meant letting this one slide into the darkest hell. So I held off letting my emotions speak reason to me.

Rain slid down the window glass, and Billy watched it like it was a thing to behold. I wondered if he was trying to take in all he could knowing he would soon be dead—that he was aware that his last hours were the most precious ones of his young life.

We ate, or at least I did, and drank coffee, something he seemed to tolerate as long as there was enough milk and sugar in it, and the rain continued falling steady on.

"You know something," he finally said. "I'd shoot you dead if I got the chance."

"I reckon you would," I said and paid the bill, and we stood and walked out into the rain and down the street to the livery.

I paid the man for boarding our horses.

"How far to Ciudad de Tontos?" I said.

"Twenty or so miles yet," he said. "The road is very bad when it rains. It will make it slow going for you. Gets very muddy."

"Thanks," I said. "Can I board the buggy here till I get back?"

"Sí, sure."

I helped the kid get aboard the horse, then got aboard my own.

"One more thing," I said to the liveryman. "There someplace I can buy a gun?"

He shrugged, said, "Sí, the trading post has guns," and pointed up the street. We walked our horses up the street to the trading post and tied them off out front.

I had my Henry rifle and mine and the Cap'n's pistols. Somehow it didn't seem enough for the job at hand.

Inside smelled like wool blankets and beef jerky, dried chilies and coffee. A young, dark-skinned woman stood behind the counter.

"Sí?" she said.

"I'll need to buy a gun," I said.

She showed me a tray of pistols.

"Something bigger—*muy grande.*"

She kept her eyes on Billy the whole while. They were compassionate eyes, but also the eyes of a woman in the market for a man. She was maybe thirty and had no wedding band on her finger.

She led us to another counter and pointed to a rack of guns and right off I spotted something I wanted. A double-barrel ten-gauge L. C. Smith.

"How much?" I said, pointing.

She took it down.

"Fifteen dollars," she said.

"I'll take it."

I paid her from the Cap'n's wallet since I was down to broke. I figured he wouldn't mind the expenditure knowing what it was for.

"You got shells for this?"

She nodded and took a box of shells off the counter behind her.

"Not these," I said. "These are for a twelve-gauge. Those." I pointed to another box and she got them for me.

I looked at Billy, who was now trading looks with the woman.

"Anything you need, kid?"

It took him a moment.

"Just to go kill that damn Mescan," he said. I saw the way she flinched. The kid lacked any social graces whatsoever.

I asked the woman if she had slickers to sell. She didn't understand my meaning. I tried to explain it but didn't know the right word. I looked around and didn't see any, but did see some serapes.

"I'll take two of those," I said, pointing. She got some down, held them up to Billy and me to gauge the right size, then I paid for them too, and we slipped them over our heads.

I thanked the woman and we went back out again, and I waited till Billy got in his saddle and handed him up the shotgun.

"Carry this," I said. "Don't worry, I wasn't stupid enough to load it."

"Then what's the point?"

"To keep you from shooting me in the back, how's that for a point."

"It ain't as if I ain't got enough to do just carrying my own damn self without having to haul this piece of iron."

"Shut your carping for once."

"Ah hell," he said.

I mounted the stud and turned him back to the south road.

The liveryman had been right about the road. The horses sank down into the mud past their fetlocks and after just a few miles they were laboring.

"We're going to have to push hard to make it to Ciudad de Tontos in two days," I said.

"This shoulder of mine is hurting like a son of a bitch," he said. "I can't ride hard even if this damn mud wasn't slowing us down."

"You stay up or I'll tie you belly down, but either way, we're going to make these next twenty or so miles by deadline."

You couldn't tell you were in Old Mexico. It

didn't look or feel any different. It was just a place where somebody had long ago decided one side of the river was the United States of America and the other the Republic of Mexico.

How the hell that got to be determined was way beyond me, and it didn't matter a spit's worth because whether I killed a man this side of the river or the other, or he killed me, dying was still dying.

"This is the worst fucking country I ever been in," Billy griped. The rain soaked through our serapes and eventually through our clothes and ran down our necks. The serapes became little more than an extra load wet like they were, but still of some unknown comfort.

"Shoulder feels like it's been cleaved with an ax," Billy said a little farther on. I kept thinking, *In a little while, kid, nothing's going to hurt you anymore.*

Chapter Twenty-Three

We rode on like that slow, the rain falling harder like nails spilled from a carpenter's barrel. The sky grew dark as night and lightning shook through it like fence wire, its flash lighting up the landscape and each other in quick bursts. I could see in those grim moments how much Billy was hurting. We slogged on still, then I heard a *whomp!* in the mud. I reined in my horse and waited till the next flash of lightning and saw Billy lying there in the road, his horse running past me, spooked by the crash of thunder. I charged off after it and finally caught it up by the reins and led it back.

I dismounted and lifted Billy from the mire.

"I'm finished," he said. "You want to tie me belly down, you're going to have to 'cause I can't ride another mile."

Then I saw with the next lightning flash his eyes had rolled white. I went and untied my soogins and wrapped it round him after I dragged him off the road into the scrub. He lay there without moving and I hunkered there on my heels, miserable and soaked to the skin. The rain hissed and boiled and took no mercy on us, and I kept thinking how much nicer it would have been to be home in my own bed with Luz's warm body wrapped against mine. I told myself that maybe I ought to make an honest woman out of her and ask her to marry me when I got back—if I got back. The idea appealed to me more than I thought it ever would. I had my share of women and ladies but none that ever made me want to marry one of them.

But a man reaches a point where he knows that whatever he's been doing all his life he can't go on forever doing. Something happens to you when you hit forty years old, it seems. And I'd hit forty sometime back.

The rain dripped down the back of my neck.

The lightning danced all around like it was looking for us to kill us. Anybody who's ever trailed cattle could tell you the danger of lightning. But still, there was nothing to be done about it.

Billy was almost dead and I wasn't feeling too spry myself.

It was a long, long damn wait sitting out there in that rainstorm, and by the time it quit, the first gray light of a new dawn cut through sky and you could have wrung our clothes out like washrags.

It took me several moments to waken the kid. But finally his eyes fluttered open like a busted shade in some cheap hotel room.

"Kid," I said. "We got to get a move on. It's Thursday. By Friday, that little brother of yours is going to be dead if we don't make it down there."

He shook his head.

"Can't . . . go . . . on . . . ," he muttered.

I lifted him onto my shoulders and heaved him into the saddle.

"You die, he dies," I said. "Is that what you want?"

He waggled his head.

"Then take hold of that saddle horn."

I mounted my horse and took up the reins to Billy's and led him out. I didn't know where we were or how far we'd come or how far we had to go. I had to carry the shotgun across the pommel of my saddle since I couldn't trust the kid to hold on to it. He was barely able to hold on himself.

We crossed a swollen creek that had come over the road, and a short way farther on we came upon a sheep camp that lay just off to our right and you could smell the cook pot and coffee.

"Let's ride over and see can we get a little something for our bellies and some of that coffee," I said. Even my bones were cold and soaked from the all-night rain.

The sheep—and there must have been nearly a hundred of them—were cropping grass contentedly as their herder squatted by the fire. He had three black and white dogs patrolling the flock.

He looked up at our approach.

I greeted him in Spanish and with a touch of my hat brim.

"Don't suppose I could buy a meal and some of that coffee from you?" I said.

He blinked, looked me over, then looked over Billy.

"Come, sit," he said.

I dismounted and helped Billy out of the saddle.

"What's wrong with your friend?"

"He's feeling poorly," I said, helping Billy to

ease to the ground by the fire. He looked worse than an orphan.

The man stood and went to his wagon and came back with two extra tin plates and cups and handed them to me and nodded to the cook pot. I spooned us out each a plate and then poured us each a cup of the coffee.

"You from around here?" I said, chewing the mutton stew.

He pointed to a line of mountains.

"Over there," he said. "Chipata."

I nodded. The coffee began to warm my blood and I was grateful for it and poured myself a second cup. It was strong and black as a crowbar.

"How's that suit you, kid?" I said. He was at least eating and sipping his coffee. He glanced my way and then across the fire at the shepherd.

"I ain't proud to be eating a Mescan's food," he said.

"You best be grateful he gave you anything to eat at all," I said. Then to the shepherd, "You'll have to forgive my young companion's manners. He ain't got any."

The shepherd laughed.

"The wild ways of the young," he said. As though he understood that boys Billy's age were tempestuous and often ignorant in their ways.

I asked if he knew how far it was yet to Ciudad de Tontos. He held up the fingers of one hand.

Smoke from the fire rose in gray wisps.

"They had some trouble down there not long ago," he said.

"What sort of trouble?" I said, believing I already knew but wanting to confirm it.

"There is a garrison of Ruales there and the General's daughter was killed, murdered by some gringos. So you better be careful when you go there. They might think you're the ones who did it."

"We're no sort of killers," I said.

"I did not think you were. A man who is so kind to a wounded boy, even a surly one, could not be a bad hombre."

The man kept his eyes on Billy when he said that. Billy did not return the man's gaze.

I reached into my pocket and took out two dollars for our meal and handed it to the shepherd. He looked at it and said, "No. This won't do me any good," and handed it back. "I would have just thrown out the extra coffee anyway and the stew, whatever is left over, I give to my dogs."

The sheep bleated whenever the dogs would nip at their legs if they strayed from the flock.

"Those look like some good dogs," I said.

"They keep me company and do a good job with the sheep."

I stood then and said, "Thank you for your hospitality. My name is Jim Glass and this is Billy Rogers."

"And I am Hernando," he said and we shook hands.

"And thanks for the warning about Ciudad de Tontos," I said.

He scratched under his sombrero.

"I think there is a doctor there who could look at the boy's arm," he said. "I think maybe he pulls teeth too if you have one that is bothering you."

"Let's mount up," I said to Billy and watched as he unscrewed himself from the ground. Got him mounted on his horse, and we headed the last five miles to the town where his death awaited him.

I felt gruesome, like a man taking a sheep to slaughter.

From what I knew of Mexican manhood, it might not be as simple as exchanging one boy for the other.

I was glad I had the ten-gauge.

Chapter Twenty-Four

Billy visibly stiffened when he saw the town rising up before us. At this distance, it seemed innocent enough. But then lots of things, women and towns and men included, seem innocent enough if you're standing a long way away from them.

"Hold your water, kid. This might not seem as bad as what you imagine it to be." I needed to do my level best to keep him calm, to keep the situation contained. Because if it got out of hand, it wasn't only the kid that might end up dead, and I sure didn't want to become a corpse in a place called City of Fools.

"How'd you know how bad it's not going to be," he groused. "Anybody ever kill you before? Especially some goddamn Mescan Ruale."

"You got a point, kid. I wouldn't know. But I made your grandfather a promise, and I aim to see it through."

"Least give me a gun, give me a fighting chance."

"You think having a gun would give you a fighting chance against a company of Ruales?"

"It'd be something."

"Something is all it *would* be."

"How you know they're not going to kill us all, you included?"

"I don't. But if what your grandfather said about him and the General being pals back in the old days is true, maybe he'll cut some slack for your brother."

"Yeah, and maybe that sum bitch won't either."

"Chance we'll have to take," I said, feeling about as uneasy as I've ever felt riding into an uncertain situation with the only promise being that there'd be some bloodletting.

I saw a man packing a burro and paused and said, "*Dónde está la oficina de los* Ruales?"

He was tying a diamond hitch on a load that looked like all the burro could stand.

He pointed up the street and said in Spanish that the Ruales were located mid-block center of town. I thanked him and spurred my mount ahead, still leading Billy's by the reins. He seemed resigned to his fate when I last looked back at him.

There were Ruales standing out front of the General's office in tan uniforms when we rode up. Billy said, "The jail's in back."

The Ruales were smoking, talking about something, but stopped when we reined in. One of them seemed to recognize Billy and quick ran inside and returned in a moment with a rifle in his hands and the General on his heels. His hair was uncommonly black for a man his age. His mustaches guarded the corners of his mouth and down past his chin.

"What's this?" he said with feigned surprise as he stared at Billy.

"I've come on behalf of Gus Rogers," I said. "You remember Gus Rogers, don't you, General?"

He looked at me with a baleful stare, then signaled to his men, who stepped forward to take Billy off his horse.

"Not yet," I said, raising the shotgun from where it had been resting across my pommel to let the stock rest atop my right thigh. "Tell your men to hold off."

He raised a hand.

"He is my prisoner," he said. "He escaped from my jail after murdering my child."

"He will be in your jail once again after we make the exchange for the one you're holding—young Sam Rogers."

The General got a look on his face as if someone had just whispered something pleasant in his ear.

"Where is my old friend Gus?" he said.

"Dead and buried north of here, not far if you want to pay him a visit—little town called Gonzales. Ask for the German, he'll show you the grave."

The smile dropped away.

"Did you kill him?"

"No, he killed himself."

The smile that had gone away turned into a frown.

"This I find hard to believe, a man like him," he said.

"Believe what you will. He asked me to fulfill his mission if he couldn't. That's why I'm here instead of back home in a warm bed with a full belly of beef."

"What is your name?"

"Not that it makes any difference," I said. "But it's Jim Glass. I'm not here for a social visit. Let's get this done if we're going to do it."

"First you give me him, then I will give you the other one," he said.

"No, that's not how this is going to work."

He snorted his derision.

"Who are you to dictate the terms? I have

205

enough men here to kill you and take him. You're just one man."

I leveled the L. C. ten-gauge so that the thick black barrels were aimed directly at the General's chest. And when I thumbed back the hammers, it gave you the same feeling you get when you're walking through the brush and hear the buzz of a rattlesnake real close and you're not sure where it's at, whether you've taken one step too many.

"That's true," I said. "I am only one man, but I'm man enough to take you and some of these Ruales out with me if that's what you want. You can go get that boy or go to fighting."

The Ruales around him shuffled their feet nervously till he waved them to stand still.

He showed me both his palms.

"I done what you asked the Cap'n to do," I said. "I brought you this boy in exchange for the other one. Now let's trade or let's do whatever it is you've got in mind, but I'm not sitting here all day in this fucking hot sun."

He looked at those empty black holes of the L. C. and I guess it made him rethink his plans just as it surely would mine if he was holding that bad gun instead of me. Finally he assented with the dip of his head toward one of his men.

"Go and get the boy," he said.

"One more thing," I said.

He held his chin at a stately angle, raised so that now he was looking down his nose at me.

"That boy needs some medical attention. I expect you to do whatever it is you're planning to do with some sense of decency."

"All matters will be done with proper attention," he said. He might as well have said Queen Victoria ruled England, for all the difference it would make.

The kid they brought out was smallish, baby-faced, and in a stupor till he looked up and saw Billy astraddle the horse.

"Billy . . . ," he uttered.

"Sam. They're swapping me for you. This fellow will take you home. You're safe now."

"No," Sam said. "I'm not going to leave you."

Billy got down off his horse gritting his teeth and said, "Go on now, get away from here and this dirty business. Do it before something upsets the applecart."

Sam began to sob.

"Be a man," Billy said sternly. "I taught you anything, it was to be a man. Now git."

The General and his Ruales stood watching, listening, waiting for a mistake to be made. You been doing what I've done most of my life, you can tell if a man is full of bad intentions. It wouldn't take much to start a shooting scrap that would leave the sidewalks bloody and several of us dead. But I had no choice, I was already in it too deep to do anything other than stand my ground.

"Get on the horse, Sam," I said.

"No."

"Get on the goddamn horse, boy."

"Go on," Billy said again, pushing Sam toward the horse. "Go and tell Ma what happened here. Take care of her, Sam. I'm sorry I got you into all this."

Sam did a slow shuffle to the horse.

"Hurry it along there, kid," I said. The air was so thick with men wanting to let blood, you could cut it with a knife.

The Ruales took Billy in hand.

"There, you see," General Toro said. "We are both men who keep our promises, eh."

I gave Billy one last glance. He stared at me without a hint of worry in his gaze. I said to Sam without taking my eyes or the double barrels off the General, "Ride up the street that way, and don't dawdle. Ride fast and I'll catch up with you. Don't stop and don't turn around. And if something bad happens, keep riding till you cross the river and don't even stop then."

"Yes sir," he uttered and kicked his horse into a trot, then a gallop.

It left me, the General, and five of his Ruales—what you call a Mexican showdown, only I wasn't wanting to turn this into something bloody.

"Then our business is finished," the General said.

"It's finished," I said and backed my horse up

far enough, then reined it round quick and spurred it into a full-out gallop.

Nobody took a shot at me. I was a little surprised they hadn't.

I caught up quickly enough with the little brother, whose horse was a lot less horse than the stud.

"Hold up!" I shouted, and he sawed back on the reins.

"I thought you told me to keep riding?"

"I did. But now I want you to stop a second."

He looked at me with the confusion of a boy who'd just escaped death and couldn't understand why.

"What'd they do to you back there in that jail?" I said.

"Beat me like blue blazes . . ."

"What else?"

"Said they were going to shoot me, made me watch them execute the man who let Billy escape. They brought in the General's wife and she spit in my face. Kept telling me how my day was coming, how I'd bawl like a woman when it was my turn."

"That's if they didn't get Billy back, right?"

He shook his head.

"Said they'd get Billy and kill us both, and Granddaddy too if he put up a fuss. They wasn't ever planning on letting me live."

"You certain that's what they said?"

"I swear to God, mister."

"One more question, boy. Did you or your brother have anything to do whatsoever with the death of the General's girl?"

"No sir. We found her stabbed and Billy and me did the best we could to save her. We had her blood all over us, but it wasn't because we were trying to hurt her none."

It was the same story Billy had told. They could have gotten together and made it up, but I doubted it; neither of them seemed that clever.

"You think you can reach the river on your own? You just have to stay on this road and keep going."

He nodded.

"What about you?" he said.

"I got something I need to do." I took out Gus's watch, wallet, and badge and handed them to him along with Gus's fancy pistol.

"These belonged to your granddaddy," I said.

"Where's my granddaddy at?"

"North of here, buried in the ground. He did what he could for you, he just ran out of time."

"I hardly remember him," he said.

"You have your mama tell you about him when you get home again. First town you hit that has a train station, you sell that horse and use the money and some of what's in that wallet and buy you a ticket home. You understand?"

"Yes sir."

"And don't ever come back across that river again—leastways till you're a man and can make up your own mind."

"Yes sir."

I slapped the rump of his horse, shouting, "Git," and sat until I saw he wasn't going to stop again. Then I turned the stud back around.

Shit, I was almost forty-six years old and not getting any younger and there was this kid in a jail they were going to shoot over nothing at all.

I just couldn't ride away from that. Even though I should, I couldn't.

Chapter Twenty-Five

As if it were some sort of Greek tragedy, the kind I'd seen performed in Dodge City when I was a young buckaroo, the sky grew ominously dark again, and raindrops the size of silver dollars splatted down, a few at first, then more, smaller but more intense as I rode back toward the town of Ciudad de Tontos.

But I thought the only fool in this whole business was me.

I rode at a walk, steady, determined, the stock of the shotgun resting against my thigh, both hammers cocked, ready to do some mean business if required, and it surely would be this day before the sun set again beyond those stormy clouds.

The storm had chased everyone indoors, and as I rode past the business establishments I could see faces looking out—clerks, bankers, hardware salesmen, men in the cantina standing in the open doorway under the shelter of a roof, leaning there with their bottles and glasses in their hands. Men in tall sombreros stood under the eaves with the rain dripping off, some of them held glasses of beer like it was a show.

I rode down past the first block of buildings, a stable with a corral with no horses in it; a blacksmith's whose forge showered sparks as he fired the steel; a gunsmith's with a CERRADO sign in the window. The old man who had been packing his burro stood in the rain, his serape heavy and wet about his shoulders, looked directly into my eyes as if he knew what was about to happen. He turned, untied his burro from the hitching post, and walked the other direction.

I crossed the only intersection in town, Segunda Calle—Second Street—and kept my attention fixed ahead. I saw a kid standing under the eaves in front of a barbershop. He stared at me like I was the devil incarnate, or Jesus Christ himself. He was a kid that would someday, if he was lucky, grow to be a man, maybe even an old man. I reined in and told him to get off the street. He was hesitant to go. I gave him two bits. He ran like hell.

I tied off the stud. The Ruale office was just across the street two doors down. I could see lights on inside. I didn't want to think what they were doing to Billy.

I had the shotgun and I had a pistol and either I'd get the job done or I wouldn't.

Rain fell out of the black heavens.

I crossed the street.

I didn't bother to knock. I just turned the knob and went in fast.

The General and two of his Ruales were sitting there drinking from a bottle of tequila. I leveled the ten-gauge.

They all looked surprised.

"I come to get the kid," I said.

The General looked at me with a great amount of empathy.

"You already have him," he said evenly.

"The other one—Billy," I said.

"Oh, but that is not possible," he said. I had to admit, the son of a bitch was a cool customer, showed no fear whatsoever. The other two weren't quite so calm. I could see the fear in their eyes and they had every right to be afraid.

"Yes, it is possible," I said. "Nobody has to get killed here. That boy didn't have anything to do with your daughter's death."

"So you say, Señor. But you see, my men here, they caught him with her blood on him. And he has confessed to as much. There is no injustice here, no reason for you to act like this. Gus, he would have understood it—what a man must do to remove the stain of dishonor from his family name."

"I'm saying he's innocent. Now let's go and get him out of your goddamn jail."

Still, the General did not make any move to do as ordered. I looked at one of the two with him—the one who showed the most fear—and said, "You want to live, you son of a bitch?"

I could tell he didn't understand so I said it again in Spanish so he would understand: "*Usted desea vivir usted hijo de una perra?*"

"Sí, sí."

So I told him to get the keys and go get the kid.

He started to but the General ordered him to halt. Told him who did he think his boss was, the General or me? The Ruale looked caught between a rock and a hard place, which is exactly where he was.

I moved a step and put the barrels of the L. C. right against his neck.

"Do it!" I said.

"You think even if we give you the boy we're going to just let you ride across the river to del Norte?" the General said. "We will hunt you down like rabbits."

"I'll take my chances."

He motioned for one of the Ruales to get the keys and he opened a desk drawer, and I told him to come out easy, and he did with a large key on a metal ring. I marched all three to the back of the place where Billy lay on his side on the cot.

"Get up," I said.

For some reason he didn't seem surprised to see me. He eased himself up holding his busted shoulder.

"I didn't think no kind of man who was a friend of my granddaddy would just ride off and let these Mescan sons of bitches murder me," he said with a whoop as if he'd just won first prize in a pie-eating contest.

I told the Ruale to open the door, intending to put the three of them inside while the kid and me got a jump start on them, but just then three more Ruales came busting through the door with pistols cocked and ready and I didn't have any choice but to pull the triggers of that L. C., knocking them down like tenpins. The L. C. roared like thunder in that small room, so loud it made your ears ring. But just that quick the General and his two boys were all over me before I could pull my pistol and I knew if they got me to the ground, it was all over.

I slammed an elbow into one face and threw a crushing right-hand fist into the face of the other. But the General had a hard grip on me, his forearm from behind around my throat, trying to choke me out. He was a strong son of a bitch, I'll give him that, and we fought out into the other room, mostly him choking and me trying to break his grip.

I heard Billy yell something and a struggle still going on inside the cell area, but I had my hands too full to help him. He was on his own now.

My wind cut off, I was starting to lose my strength, which only encouraged the General to choke down that much harder. I had maybe thirty seconds before I'd go under.

I took him out through the plate-glass window with one mighty push, hoping to break his grip.

We crash landed on the wet walk outside and rolled into the muddy street and it momentarily loosened his chokehold on me enough so I could gasp some air. I reached for my pistol, but it wasn't in the scabbard. I'd lost it somewhere in the struggle.

I heard three sharp reports from inside the office—gunfire!

It was then I looked up and was staring down the barrel of the General's own pistol—a nickel-plated Smith & Wesson Russian model, like the one the Cap'n carried, and I wondered stupidly if theirs had been a matched set and where and when and how they'd come by them.

Funny what a man who's an instant away from death will think. I always heard your life flashed before your eyes and sometimes you saw the presence of loved ones who'd passed before.

But all I saw was a tall man in a muddy uniform

standing there with his gun aimed at my face, saw him thumb back the hammer and thought, *Jim, you're going to die here in this muddy goddamn street and not in a nice bed like you'd planned.*

Then an explosion caused the General to jerk like someone had snipped all his wires, and he fell face-first into the mud dead as a stone.

Standing there a dozen paces behind where the General lay was the little brother, Sam, holding his granddaddy's pistol, the one that matched the General's in every detail.

He did not move or falter.

And when Billy came straggling out of the jail holding one of the *federale*'s pistols in his good hand, smoke curling from the barrel, I knew then old Gus's blood had passed on down to those boys in spite of everything else.

We rode north, the three of us, Billy, Sam, and myself.

We did not dally, for to be north of the river was to be safe again.

At least for a little while.

Chapter Twenty-Six

She was there at the house, my house, waiting for me as if she knew I'd come. She was stroking the muzzle of one of the mares, and it pricked its ears at our approach, and the stud whinnied smelling the mare, his muscles rippled, as glad to be home again as I was.

Luz turned and did not move but stood watching, and my heart quickened at the sight of her.

I rode up casual as if I'd been gone on a Sunday ride, but she could see my overall condition was pretty poor, my clothes dusty and mud-caked, my shirt sweat-stained and my boots all run down.

I reined in and stepped down out of the saddle.

She did not speak and I did not speak. I unsaddled the stud and turned him out with the mares.

"You earned it," I said. Then I turned to Luz and said, "How you been getting on?"

"Fine," she said. "And yourself."

"Been better," I said. "Am better now that I'm home again."

I saw my chicken coop was rebuilt and the

fencing put up and some of the chickens put back inside, and that old red rooster that would wake me up every morning about the time it got light.

"You do that?" I said, pointing toward the chicken coop.

"Who else do you think would trouble themselves to round up your chickens and fence them in again?"

"Nobody I know but you."

"That's right, mister, and don't you forget it."

I took her in my arms then and gave her a hug and kissed her on the mouth like it was the first time—tenderly and gratefully.

"I've got some coffee on," she said.

"I'd rather just sit out here and have a whiskey with you, and a smoke."

"That can be arranged," she said and went into the house and came out with the bottle and two glasses, and we sat in chairs facing off to the west where the sun was setting a passionate red in the sky, throwing off its light up against fingers of clouds. I rolled her a shuck and rolled myself one, and we sat there smoking and sipping our whiskey.

"You want to talk about it?" she said at last.

"No, I don't reckon," I said.

"I half thought you'd show up with your friend," she said.

"I left him down there in that country," I said.

She didn't ask which country I meant and I didn't volunteer it. It was enough to know the Cap'n was at rest now, that his two grandsons were home with their mother, and that what he set out to do got done. It didn't really matter which of us had done what. A mama had her boys back—that's what mattered.

"You hungry?" she said. "I can fix you something to eat."

"I am," I said.

She started to stand to go into the house.

"But not for food," I said.

She turned and smiled and sat down on my lap.

"Oh," she said. "Am I to guess what you're hungry for?"

"This," I said.

The sun dropped out of the sky, the heat went with it. The land grew cool and pleasant all around us.

I said, "You know that little lake over yonder the river flows out of?"

"Yes, what about it?"

I don't think she ever looked as beautiful to me as she did in that moment.

"Let's go over there and take our clothes off and jump in," I said.

"Really?" she said, arching her eyebrow.

"Yes, I had this dream while I was gone, about you and me making love in the water, and I'd like to see if it would be as good in reality as it was in that dream I had, because that was about the best old dream I ever had."

She stood and took me by the hand.

And I followed willingly.

About the Author

Bill Brooks is the author of nineteen novels of historical and frontier fiction. He lives in North Carolina.

Center Point Large Print
600 Brooks Road / PO Box 1
Thorndike ME 04986-0001 USA

(207) 568-3717

US & Canada:
1 800 929-9108
www.centerpointlargeprint.com